"Your Father Wants A Dynastic Marriage. Real But—"

"Loveless," she finished for him before he could spell it out for her.

He nodded. "It's been done for centuries."

Of course, it was centuries of ruthless breeding that had produced Sawyer Langsford—a man's man, a captain of industry, a guy who seemed capable of impregnating a woman just by looking at her.

"I'm suggesting a short-term arrangement for our mutual benefit," Sawyer stated.

"Well, I know what you would get out of the arrangement," she shot back.

"Do you?" he said smoothly.

Dear Reader,

I've always wanted to write a series with aristocratic grooms. This one draws upon my wonderful New York City as well as the English countryside, which I grew to love while studying abroad after college.

I hope you're entertained (and have a laugh or two) while reading Tamara and Sawyer's romance. It was fun watching my tart-tongued, nonconformist heroine loosen up the conservative (or so she thinks) hero. Tamara may have made a devil's bargain, but Sawyer may wind up losing his heart!

I also hope you enjoy reading about Tamara and Sawyer's friends—Pia and Belinda, and Hawk and Colin. Watch for their stories, coming soon from Silhouette Desire!

Warmly,

Anna

ANNA DePALO

HIS
BLACK SHEEP
BRIDE

Silhouette® Desire

Published by Silhouette Books
America's Publisher of Contemporary Romance

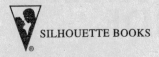 SILHOUETTE BOOKS

ISBN-13: 978-0-373-73047-6

Recycling programs
for this product may
not exist in your area.

HIS BLACK SHEEP BRIDE

Visit Silhouette Books at www.eHarlequin.com

Printed in U.S.A.

Books by Anne DePalo

Silhouette Desire

ANNA DePALO

A former intellectual property attorney, Anna DePalo lives with her husband, son and daughter in New York City. Her books have consistently hit the Waldenbooks bestseller list and Nielsen BookScan's list of top 100 bestselling romances. Her books have won an *RT Book Reviews* Reviewers' Choice Award for Best First Series Romance and have been published in over a dozen countries. Readers are invited to surf to www.annadepalo.com, where they can join Anna's mailing list.

For Olivia

One

Serving as maid of honor at a wedding was hard enough. If you were trying to avoid someone—such as your intended fiancé—it could be unbearable.

From across The Plaza's crowded reception room, Tamara eyed Sawyer Langsford—or as he was more grandly known in some quarters, the Twelfth Earl of Melton.

She reflected that some things—say, an uncaged lion—were best considered at a distance. Sawyer was an unpleasant reminder of the match her father and his had given voice to making for years. And then, Sawyer had never vocalized *his* thoughts about marrying her, leaving her in a perpetual state of unease.

If she was wary and even hostile, it was also because her personality and Sawyer's were so different—he being so much like her tradition-bound but ambitious, aristocratic father.

Damn Sawyer for being here today. Didn't he have a drafty English castle somewhere that needed his attention? Or at least a moldering dungeon where he could sit and brood?

What was he doing playing the part of one of Tod Dillingham's debonair groomsmen?

If only he looked like a dark, unhappy aristocrat fighting private demons. Instead, he was all golden leonine prowess, owning his domain and topping most people in the room.

If she were being fair, she'd say a society wedding wasn't all that surprising a place for her to run into Sawyer. Almost unavoidable, really, since Sawyer spent a great deal of time in New York for his media business.

But she wasn't in the mood to be fair. Today, as Belinda Wentworth's maid of honor, she'd had to stand at the altar, a smile pasted on her face, aware of Sawyer mere feet away among the other groomsmen.

As the Episcopal priest had intoned the words that would join Belinda and Tod in wedlock, Sawyer's gaze had come to rest on her. He'd looked every inch the aristocrat in white tie and tails, his black tuxedo accentuating his masculinity and air of command. His light-brown hair had reflected gold, caught in a beam of light filtering through one of the church's stained-glass windows, as if some deity in a whimsical mood had decided to spotlight a naughty angel.

Shortly after that moment, the Wentworth-Dillingham nuptials had gone hopelessly awry.

Tamara would have been consoling Belinda at the moment, if the bride were anywhere to be found. But Belinda had disappeared along with Colin Granville, Marquess of Easterbridge—the man who had interrupted the wedding ceremony with the shocking news that his Las Vegas marriage to Belinda two years earlier had never been annulled.

Now, from across the room, Tamara watched with a sinking heart as her father, Viscount Kincaid, approached Sawyer and the two men began to chat.

After a moment, Sawyer looked across the room, and his gaze locked with hers.

His face was handsome but unyielding—the stamp of

generations of conquerors and rulers on his face. His physique was lean and solid, like a soccer star in his prime.

Just then, the side of Sawyer's mouth lifted in silent amusement, and Tamara felt her pulse pick up.

Disconcerted, she quickly looked away. She told herself her reaction had nothing to do with physical attraction, and everything to do with annoyance.

To bolster that thought, she wondered whether Sawyer had had advance notice of what Colin had intended—and perhaps more, had been feeding Colin inside information. She hadn't seen Sawyer near Colin earlier at St. Bartholomew's Church. But she'd seen them speaking at social functions in the past, so she knew them to be friendly.

Tamara's lips compressed.

Trust Sawyer to be friends with a villain like Colin Granville, Marquess of Easterbridge, who'd just acquired another title: wedding crasher extraordinaire.

She looked around, careful not to glance in Sawyer's direction. She couldn't find Pia Lumley, either. She wondered whether the wedding planner—part of her and Belinda's trio of girlfriends—had managed to catch up with the bride after encouraging all the guests to repair to a show-must-go-on reception at The Plaza. Or whether Pia was closeted somewhere, in fits over the nuptial disaster that had befallen them all today.

The last time she'd seen Pia, the pixie blonde had been walking away from James Carsdale, Duke of Hawkshire, another friend of Sawyer's, and toward the swinging doors that admitted the waitstaff. Perhaps right now someone in the kitchen was waving smelling salts under her friend's nose, trying to revive her from a dead faint.

Tamara sighed, but then her gaze landed on Sawyer again, and their eyes connected.

His mouth lifted sardonically, and then he turned his head

to exchange a few words with her father before both men glanced at her.

A moment later, she realized with horror that Sawyer and her father were heading in her direction.

For a split second, she thought about trying to get away. *Run! Duck! Disappear!*

But Sawyer was advancing on her with a mocking look in his brown eyes, and her spine straightened.

If the media baron was searching for a story, she'd give him one.

Of course, a delicious scandal had just landed in his lap with the Wentworth-Dillingham almost-wedding, but she could always add icing to the cake for him.

After all, didn't a number of his newspapers publish the pseudonymously-authored Pink Pages of Mrs. Jane Hollings—bane of society hostesses and tart-tongued nemesis of social climbers everywhere?

Tamara pressed her lips into a thin line.

"Tamara, my dear," her father said, his expression hearty, "you remember Sawyer, don't you?" He chuckled. "No introductions are necessary, I assume."

Tamara felt her face stiffen until it resembled a frozen tundra. "Quite."

Sawyer inclined his head. "Tamara…it's a pleasure. It's been a long time."

Not nearly long enough, she thought, before gesturing around them. "It looks as if you'll be the subject of your own newspapers after the wedding debacle today." She arched a brow. "Mrs. Jane Hollings is one of your columnists, isn't she?"

A ghost of a smile crossed Sawyer's lips. "I believe so."

She smiled back thinly. "I can't imagine being the topic of your own gossip would sit well with you."

His lips curved easily this time. "I don't believe in press censorship."

"How practically democratic of you."

Rather than looking offended by her jab, he seemed amused. "The earldom is hereditary, but the title of media baron was acquired in the court of public opinion."

It was on the tip of her tongue to ask what else was hereditary—his arrogance, perhaps?

Her father cleared his throat. "Let's turn to a more pleasant subject, shall we?"

"Yes, let's," she agreed.

Her father's gaze swung between her and Sawyer. "It seems like only yesterday the previous earl and I were sitting in his library, sipping fine bourbon and speculating over the happy possibility our children might one day unite our families through marriage."

There it was again. As far as hints went, it was about as subtle as a sledgehammer.

She resisted the urge to close her eyes and groan, and she was careful not to look at Sawyer.

Apparently, just as she'd feared, seeing her and Sawyer as part of the bridal party had been giving her father ideas—or rather, bringing back old ideas. *Very* old ideas.

She'd grown up hearing the story told and retold. Years ago, before Sawyer's father had passed away, her father and the Eleventh Earl of Melton had already been chummy enough to talk about a dynastic marriage between their two families—one that would unite their respective media empires, as well.

Unfortunately for her, as the eldest of three female half siblings—each the product of one of the viscount's successively brief marriages—she was the logical selection to fulfill dynastic aspirations.

And, likewise, Sawyer, as the successor to the earldom, since his father had died five years ago, was the natural choice on the other side.

Fortunately, both her younger sisters weren't in attendance

today, but instead were tucked away at their respective universities. She knew she could withstand Sawyer Langsford. She didn't want to worry about her younger and more impressionable sisters.

After all, she conceded somewhat grudgingly, Sawyer had massive appeal for the opposite sex. She'd seen evidence of that herself over the years, which served as yet another on her very long list of reasons to dislike Sawyer.

"Not that silly story again," she said, attempting to laugh off her father's words.

She looked at Sawyer for confirmation, but realized he was regarding her thoughtfully.

He nodded toward the band, which was playing a romantic tune. "Would you like to dance?"

"Are you joking?" she blurted.

He arched a brow. "Isn't it our job as members of the wedding party to make sure the show goes on?"

Well, he had her there, she admitted. She certainly had some obligations as the maid of honor. And assuming he wasn't a double agent for Colin Granville, erstwhile wedding interloper, she supposed he did, too.

"Splendid idea!" her father said. "I'm sure Tamara would be delighted."

She shot Sawyer a speaking look, but he just gestured pleasantly, as if to say, after you.

She preceded him to the dance floor.

She held herself stiffly in his arms, and the side of Sawyer's mouth quirked up in acknowledgment.

Her smooth, upswept red hair contrasted with her peaches-and-cream complexion, and the difference hinted at the dual sides of her personality: fiery, but poised.

She reminded him of the American actress with the fairy-tale role—what was her name? Amy Adams.

But with attitude. A lot of attitude. And he had a feeling

this Cinderella or Snow White wasn't waiting for a prince on a white steed to come save her.

Tamara had always marched to the beat of her own drummer. Viscount Kincaid's wild child. The bohemian jewelry designer with an apartment in Manhattan's SoHo neighborhood.

In fact, today she looked about as demure as he could ever remember her appearing. She wore a formfitting strapless ivory gown with a black satin sash.

But instead of the Kincaid family jewels, she wore a starburst necklace accented with black onyx, along with similarly styled drop earrings. He'd guess the jewelry was one of her own designs.

As she moved, a small rose tattoo peeked and disappeared above the bodice of her gown, right over the outside slope of her left breast—beckoning him, tantalizing him…reminding him why the two of them were like oil and water.

Her eyelashes swept upward, and she pinned him with a crystal-clear green gaze.

"What game are you playing?" she asked without preamble.

"Game?" he responded, his expression mild.

She looked annoyed. "My father refers to an arranged marriage, and in response, you ask me to dance?"

"Ah, that."

"I'd call that stoking the fire."

"I guess I should be relieved you aren't accusing me of a more sinister deed than asking you to dance."

She didn't seem to find his response the least bit amusing.

"Since you mention it," she said crossly, "I wouldn't be surprised if you had advance notice of Colin Granville's wedding escapade."

"Wouldn't you?" Interesting.

Their movements sent them skirting past another couple.

"Everyone knows you and the Marquess of Easterbridge are friends." She wrinkled her nose. "The aristocratic secret handshake, and all that."

He raised his eyebrows. "Colin is his own agent. And for the record, there's no secret handshake. It's a blood covenant—knives, thumbs, a full moon. You understand."

She didn't even bat an eyelash at his attempt at humor. "Your friendship doesn't extend to plotting society scandals?"

"No."

"It would help sell newspapers," she pointed out.

What would help him sell newspapers would be getting his hands on her father's media empire, he thought.

"Let's get back to the subject of my so-called game," he said smoothly. He exerted subtle pressure at the small of her back to guide them in a different direction.

"You're feeding the beast," she said emphatically.

By tacit agreement, over the years they'd avoided each other as much as possible whenever they'd had occasion to be at the same social function. The expectation of marriage had been like the white elephant in the room.

Until now.

"Maybe I want to feed the beast." He'd always tolerated the older generation's wedding machinations, but lately things had taken a different turn.

She looked startled. "You can't be serious."

He shrugged. "Why not? We'll probably both marry some-day, so why not to each other? A dynastic marriage is likely to be as good as any other."

"I have a boyfriend."

He scanned the crowd. "Really? Where's the lucky man?"

Her chin jutted out. "He could not attend today."

"Tell me you're not dating another sad sack." *What a waste.*

She gave him a withering look.

"So that's why you're attending the wedding without a date," he continued, knowing he proceeded at the risk of incurring her wrath.

"It hasn't escaped my notice you're here alone, as well," she shot back.

"Ah, but there's a reason."

Her eyes narrowed. "Which is…?"

"I'm interested in merging Kincaid News into Melton Media. Your father is happy to oblige…if I marry his daughter." He cocked his head, and then echoed Viscount Kincaid's words with mock seriousness. "'Keep everything in the family, you see.'"

Her eyes widened, and then she said something under her breath.

"Exactly," Sawyer agreed, and then his lips quirked up. "After all, look at all the trouble you and your sisters have given him so far. You've all refused to fall in line. Your father's pinning his hopes on the third generation."

The song ended, and she made to pull away from him, but he tightened his arm around her waist. He sensed her resistance for a moment, but then he swung her deftly in a semicircle as the band moved into the next song.

He wasn't ready to let her end their conversation just yet.

And then, she felt good in his arms, he admitted, as delicious curves pressed against him.

If she were anyone else, he'd have been charming her into giving him her phone number—and maybe more. He'd have looked forward to sleeping with her.

He'd have to play his cards more carefully with Tamara, but the end reward would be infinitely greater.

Tamara gave him an artificial smile. "You sound like my father. Are you sure you're not the same person?"

Sawyer returned her smile with a feral one of his own. Tamara's father was fit and trim for a man of seventy, but that's where the physical similarity between the two of them ended. However, the viscount's salt-and-pepper hair and grandfatherly visage disguised a sharp mind and cutthroat business instincts.

"We've both got the stomach for high stakes," Sawyer responded finally.

"Yes, how can I forget?" she retorted. "Business before pleasure and family."

He shook his head. "So bitter for someone whose lifestyle has been bankrolled by the family fortune."

"It's been at least a decade since I was young enough to be bankrolled, as you put it," she countered. "I support myself these days—by choice."

He raised his eyebrows. So Tamara's image of an independent woman was more than mere show.

"I think the word *bitter* applies to different circumstances— like going through three divorces," she said pointedly.

"And yet, the viscount strikes me as someone who's far from unhappy with life. In fact, he's such a romantic, he's trying to get you to walk down the aisle."

"With you?" she scoffed. "I think not."

His eyes crinkled with reluctant admiration, even if it was at his expense. "You're a blunt-spoken New Yorker."

She arched a brow. "A woman after your own heart, you mean? Don't you wish!"

"My first marriage proposal, and turned down flat."

"I'm sure it'll do no damage to your reputation," she replied. "You media tycoons do know how to spin a story."

After a moment, he gave a bark of laughter. "For the record, what makes me an undesirable marriage partner?"

"Where do I begin? Let me count the ways…"

"Give me the five-second news bite."

"I understand why my father would want a son-in-law like you…"

He looked at her inquiringly.

"You're both peers of the realm and press barons," she elaborated.

"And those are bad characteristics?"

"But I also know why I don't want a husband like you," she went on without answering him. "You're too much like my father."

Back to that topic, were they? "Would it help to point out I don't have three ex-wives?"

She shook her head. "You're wedded to your media empire. The news business is your first love. You live and breathe for wheeling and dealing."

"I suppose the existence of ex-girlfriends isn't enough proof to the contrary?" he asked wryly.

"And what reduced them to ex status?" she probed.

He cocked a brow. "Maybe things just didn't work out."

"The key word there being *work*," she returned. "Namely yours, I assume. My father lives and breathes the media business, even at the expense of people who love him."

He let the conversation lapse then, since it was clear they were at loggerheads. She hadn't said it, but it was clear she included herself among the victims who'd fallen by the wayside on the road of her father's ambition.

They danced in silence, but from time to time he glanced down at her averted face as she scanned the dancing and milling guests, looking as if she was searching for some escape.

She was quite a challenge. She was obviously marked by her parents' long-ago divorce and her father's overweening ambition, and unwilling to repeat her parents' mistakes.

He might have admired her unwillingness to sell herself short in the romance department. But as it happened, in these circumstances, he was the man who was being judged as not quite up to snuff.

With little effort, Tamara evoked all his latent ambivalence. He himself was the product of an ill-fated marriage between a British lord and an American socialite. So he had firsthand experience with free-spirited women who didn't adapt well to marrying into the tradition-bound British aristocracy.

His mother had named him after Mark Twain's most famous character, for God's sake. Who'd ever heard of a British earl named for someone conjured by a quintessential American author?

For a moment, Tamara made him doubt what he needed to do in order to get his hands on Viscount Kincaid's media holdings.

Then his jaw hardened. He'd be damned if he'd worked this hard to get to where he was only to be stymied by a few inconvenient conditions—including the existence of a sad-sack boyfriend.

When the music faded away, Tamara made to pull away, and he let her break free of his hold.

"We're done," she said, a challenge in her voice.

He let one side of his mouth quirk up. "Not nearly, but it's been a pleasure so far."

He watched as her green eyes widened. Then she whirled away and stalked off.

Two

The three-way conference call might as well have been invented for the girlfriend gab fest, Tamara thought.

She'd just dialed Belinda and Pia from her office phone. After Saturday's wedding disaster, she'd held off on calling. It was somewhat uncharacteristic behavior for her after a girlfriend crisis, but the truth was she'd been nursing a proverbial hangover herself. Plus, let's face it, this wasn't any old run-of-the-mill crisis involving men, money or bad bosses. It wasn't every day a woman had a bomb land on her wedding in the form of a heretofore unknown husband.

But now it was Monday morning. It was past time, Tamara thought, that she checked in and saw how her friends were holding up.

"Well, Mrs. Hollings is all over this one," she began without preamble after putting her girlfriends on speaker phone. "I swear if I ever get my hands on that woman…"

The thought that the old dragon of gossip was in Sawyer's employ only made her more irate.

Turning her mind in a different direction, she softened her tone. "Are you okay, Belinda?"

"I'll live through this," her friend responded. "I think."

"Are you still, ah, married to Colin Granville?" Pia asked, voicing the question Tamara herself wanted to ask.

"I'm afraid so," Belinda admitted. "But not for long. Just as soon as I get the *marquess*—" she stressed Colin's title sarcastically "—to agree to a valid annulment, everything will be all right."

"A quick end to a quick marriage…" Pia said brightly before trailing off uncertainly.

None of them needed a reminder of Belinda's ill-fated run to a Las Vegas wedding chapel.

Tamara knew that the Wentworths and Granvilles had been neighbors and rivals in the Berkshire countryside for generations. It was likely why Belinda had wanted her marriage to the Marquess of Easterbridge undone quietly, and had kept mum to everyone, including even her closest girlfriends, about the apparently short-lived elopement.

"Colin isn't giving you a hard time about the annulment, is he?" Tamara asked.

"Of course not!" Belinda replied. "Why would he? After all, it's not as if we had a real marriage. We dashed into a Las Vegas wedding chapel. The next morning we regretted our mistake. Colin said he'd take care of the annulment!"

"Let's back up to the part where you went into the chapel," Tamara said drily. "How did it happen? You dash to the airport to avoid missing a flight. You dash into a supermarket for some milk."

"You might even dash into Louis Vuitton to grab their latest it bag," Pia suggested.

"Exactly," Tamara went on. "But you do not dash into a wedding chapel to get hitched on the fly."

Belinda sighed. "You do if it's Vegas, and you've just run

into someone…unexpected. And you've had a drink or two that have gone straight to your head."

Pia's groan of commiseration sounded over the phone.

Tamara wondered how much blame to place on a couple of drinks, and how much on Colin himself. Her meticulous friend wasn't the type to get tipsy, at least not without a reason.

"You didn't change your name to Granville, did you?" Tamara asked. "Because if you did—"

Pia gasped. "Oh, Belinda, tell me you didn't! Tell me you didn't legally become one of the enemy!"

"Not to mention you would have been misrepresenting yourself as Belinda Wentworth for the past two years," Tamara commented.

She cringed for her friend. It looked as if Belinda, who was always so self-possessed, had dug herself a hole.

"Don't worry, I didn't change my last name," Belinda responded drily.

"So it was okay to marry a Granville, but not to become one?" Tamara quipped. "I love the way the tipsy you thinks."

"Thanks," Belinda retorted. "And don't worry—the tipsy me is not getting out of her locked and padded cell again."

Tamara laughed, but then quickly sobered. What was it about a man with a title that made a woman lose her head? Her thoughts drifted to Sawyer, and then, annoyed with herself, she focused on the topic at hand again.

Among their trio of friends, Belinda had always been the levelheaded, responsible one. After getting her degree in the history of art from Oxford, she'd begun a respectable career working at a series of auction houses. Tamara just couldn't picture Belinda eloping in Vegas with her family's nemesis. Pia, maybe, Belinda, no.

"There wasn't an Elvis impersonator involved, by chance, was there?" she heard herself ask.

Pia stifled a giggle.

"No!" Belinda said. "And I just want this headache to disappear!"

"Not likely," Tamara remarked. "I don't see Colin going away quietly."

"He will," Belinda replied adamantly. "What would make him want to stay in this ridiculous marriage?"

Now there was the million-dollar question, Tamara thought. Belinda sounded as if she was trying to convince herself as much as anyone else.

Tamara decided to turn the conversation in a different direction, to take the pressure off Belinda.

"Pia, I saw you stalking off to the kitchen at one point," she said. "You looked upset."

"I wasn't upset about Colin crashing the wedding," Pia responded. "Well, I was upset for Belinda. But I had s-someone—ah, other things on my mind."

Pia's slight stutter was in evidence, and Tamara knew it only came out these days when her friend was agitated about something.

Tamara decided to probe delicately. "Ah, Pia…these other things wouldn't have anything to do with a certain very toff British duke-turned-financier, would it?"

Pia gasped. "That didn't make Mrs. Hollings's column, too, did it?"

"I'm afraid so, sweetie."

Pia moaned. "I'm doomed."

According to the Jane Hollings column that had appeared in Sawyer's newspaper that morning, there had been an argument at Belinda's wedding reception between Pia and the Duke of Hawkshire. Reportedly, Pia had discovered at the reception that the duke was none other than the man she'd known only as Mr. James Fielding when she'd been involved with him a few years before. Upon the discovery of how she'd been mislead, Pia had apparently smashed some hors d'oeuvres into the duke's face.

"Pia, please," Belinda said, obviously trying to lighten the mood. "Doomed is committing bigamy."

"Which you didn't!"

"Almost."

"N-no one will want to hire a wedding planner who's a security risk to wealthy and titled guests!" Pia wailed.

"Did you really sleep with Hawkshire?" Belinda asked.

"He was Mr. Fielding at the time!"

"Oh, Pia."

"Oh, sweetie," Tamara said at the same time.

Naturally, Tamara thought darkly, Sawyer was friends with the duke as well as with Belinda's yet-to-be-annulled husband. Of course both of Sawyer's good friends would be disreputable.

"Well, it seems like we all had a *great* wedding," Tamara said. "Sorry, Belinda."

A sigh sounded over the phone. "No apologies necessary," Belinda said. "Not even the best spin doctor could put a good face on Saturday's disaster. It's not every day a bride almost acquires two husbands."

They all shared in some self-conscious laughter.

"Well, what made Saturday so bad for you, Tamara?" Belinda asked.

"In short?"

"Yes."

"Sawyer Langsford. Lord Odious himself."

Pia giggled.

"Oh, I don't think Sawyer is so terrible," Belinda remarked.

"Putting aside his friendship with Colin, you mean?" Tamara asked.

"Okay, I see your point," Belinda conceded.

"Sawyer is good-looking," Pia said. "Those topaz eyes, and all that rich, burnished hair—"

Tamara made a face. "Whose side are you on?"

"Well, yours."

"Good."

"What about Sawyer's presence put you out?" Belinda asked. "You've socialized before without any problem, as far as I could tell."

"Because we've always ignored each other," Tamara replied. "But my father seeing the both of us in the wedding procession reminded him of the cherished idea that he and the previous earl had of having their children marry each other."

Pia spluttered. "You and Sawyer?"

"Hilarious, I know," Tamara responded.

"Oh, rats," Belinda said. "If I'd known, I'd have suggested to Tod that he pick another groomsman."

Tamara grimaced. "It's not something I like to talk about. In fact, it's an idea I've been hoping was dead and buried. But then Sawyer made it clear on Saturday that he's willing to entertain the idea."

Pia and Belinda gasped.

Exactly, Tamara thought.

When she'd heard Sawyer was to be in the wedding party, she'd figured she was a big enough girl to handle it. But she hadn't foreseen Sawyer's proposal.

"You and Sawyer are so different!" Pia said. "You're the Bridget Jones to his Mr. Darcy."

Tamara closed her eyes in existential pain. "Please. Bridget and Darcy ended up together."

"Oops, sorry!"

Tamara knew Pia was a romantic. Being a wedding planner suited her friend's personality. The only surprising thing was that Pia herself wasn't married. But then, Pia had had her own experience with an odious man.

"So what's next for you two?" Tamara asked, wanting to change the subject.

"I'm flying to England for a few days on business."

"And I'll be in Atlanta to consult with a client on a wedding."

"Abandoning the field of battle?" Tamara couldn't resist joking.

"Never!" Belinda declared.

"In a sense," Pia said at the same time.

"I'm regrouping and marshalling my forces," Belinda went on, "including getting a lawyer."

"In meantime," Pia said, "I'll be coming up with some spectacular ideas for Belinda's second act as a bride." She added uncertainly, "Or should I say, third act…?"

There was a pause as everyone seemed to wince.

Then Tamara noticed a light flashing on her phone. "On that note, I think I have a call coming in."

As Tamara ended the call with Belinda and Pia, she wondered for which of the three of them Saturday would prove to be most portentous.

Her parting exchange with Sawyer came back to her.

She'd told him they were done, and he, damn him, had just replied insouciantly, "Not nearly, but it's been a pleasure so far."

One week later, Tamara wondered at her rotten luck.

Sawyer, again.

Usually she ran into him only once every few months. Maybe a couple of times a year.

But here he was—at a big fashion party taking place in a large TriBeCa loft. Minor celebrities, socialites and journalists were here to appreciate an up-and-coming designer.

But what was Sawyer doing here?

Tamara had seen a reporter for Sawyer's newspaper, *The New York Intelligencer,* at the party. Sawyer's own presence certainly was not necessary.

She knew he attended his share of parties, but this one was not the type he usually attended. Last time she checked, he didn't have a particular interest in fashion. In fact, she was sure his suits came from an old and stuffy Savile Row tailor with a warrant from the queen.

Sawyer's presence was a reason to keep up her guard, but at least she had body armor tonight in the form of a date.

She looked around. Tom hadn't yet returned with their drinks.

As she scanned the room, however, she noticed Sawyer walking toward her.

Rats.

She turned, but just as she ducked behind the heavy velvet curtain that encircled the perimeter of the room—obviously in place to hide blank walls and elevator doors from the view of the assembled guests—a familiar voice reached her.

"Leaving the field of battle?"

She halted, irritated that his words echoed her own to Belinda, but unwilling to show him any reaction.

Squaring her shoulders, she swung back toward him. "Never."

He gave a predatory smile. "Good."

She waved her hand toward the curtain to indicate the crowd on the other side. "I was simply trying to avoid getting blood on the designer labels in our latest skirmish."

"Thoughtful of you."

She tilted her lips in the semblance of a smile. "You might try it sometime."

After a moment, he had the indecency to chuckle.

"What are you doing here?" she blurted.

"I received an invitation, I accepted."

She frowned. "I've never seen you at a fashion event before."

"There's always a first time. Otherwise life would be boring."

She felt heat stain her cheeks, and shook off the feeling he was making a sexual suggestion about her…them.

"I suppose," she responded coolly, "though I also know there are certain things I don't care to try."

She tried to ignore the fact that her pulse had begun to skitter and skip the minute she'd heard his deep voice resonating behind her.

Her reaction both puzzled and annoyed her. Was it because he'd admitted to entertaining the idea of wedding her? It was only that she felt pursued, she insisted to herself. Surely she hadn't sunk so low as to feel flattered by his attention.

This was Sawyer, the man she'd spent a lifetime avoiding and disdaining. She wasn't like some medieval bride, content to be betrothed from birth.

Still, she couldn't help noticing he made his own fashion statement of sorts tonight. He looked model-perfect in a tieless tan suit and open-collar green shirt. It was about as fashion-forward as she could ever remember him looking. Had it been a long while since her recent encounters with Sawyer, or had he begun relaxing his sartorial standards and she simply hadn't noticed?

As if conducting his own wardrobe assessment, Sawyer gave her a sweeping look that ran up from her peep-toe slingbacks to her knee-length sheath dress, held up by spaghetti straps.

His eyes paused for a moment at her chest, before he raised them to her annoyed expression. "A redhead who isn't afraid to wear red. You never disappoint."

"I'm so glad you approve!" She couldn't help feeling there was an element of disapproval in his words. He was of her father's world, after all. Bohemian jewelry designers didn't fit.

In the next instant, however, he surprised her by reaching out to tuck a strand of hair behind her ear.

She stilled as he paused to finger a teardrop peridot earring. The contact was intimate—erotic, even—though he wasn't touching her directly.

"I'm interested in having some jewelry pieces designed," he said, his deep voice sending an involuntary thrill through her.

Pushing aside how very aware of him she was, she asked, making her voice sugary, "For your current love interest?"

He took his time answering. "You could say that."

She looked at him with exaggerated disbelief. "Am I to assume that's why you arranged to intercept me at a fashion event? Because you're looking for a jewelry designer?"

"Among other things."

She held on to her irritation because it was easier to deal with than how disturbing his nearness was. "Let's get back to what you're doing here. Or should I say, how you knew I'd be here?"

He gave her a level look. "One guess."

"My father," she said flatly.

"Correct."

Her lips tightened. "When I see him again…"

She castigated herself now for revealing to her father some of the details of her social and business schedule in response to his seemingly casual questions a couple of weeks ago when they'd met for lunch.

No question she and her father needed to have a serious conversation. One that included the reasons why he shouldn't interfere in her life. It apparently wasn't enough she was based in New York and he was often in London, putting the breadth of the Atlantic Ocean between them.

Sawyer regarded her with an unreadable expression. "Marriage is not such a crazy idea."

"Don't tell me you're still considering this!"

"The idea has its merits."

"And here I was thinking you sought me out to have a trinket designed for your current flame! Instead, you hauled yourself here in order to make a marriage proposal. Now there's a good, solid reason to attend a froufrou fashion event, when everyone knows you have zero interest in fashion!"

Thank goodness they were in a semiprivate area of the room, Tamara thought. The last thing she needed was for their argument to be witnessed by avid onlookers.

"Are you done?" he asked, his topaz eyes glittering.

Not by a mile. "How efficient of you. Well, you can erase the marriage proposal from your BlackBerry calendar! Good luck with the rest of your day."

She turned away, but she'd taken only two steps when he grasped her arm and swung her back toward him.

"You have to be the most prickly woman I know," Sawyer muttered.

"Yet another reason I wouldn't make a suitable wife," she flung back. "I can bring home the sarcasm, serve up your ego in a pan and never let you forget you're a—"

"Damn."

In the next moment, Sawyer's lips came down on hers. Tamara stilled.

Sawyer's lips were soft but firm, and in the next instant, Tamara became aware that he tasted sweet but heady and carried the warm scent of man.

Sensation coursed through her, and her body hummed to life. She'd been kissed before, of course, but kissing Sawyer, she was discovering, was like doing vodka shots when she was used to beer.

Time slowed. She felt the heavy thump of her heart, and became aware of his lean, muscular strength pressed against her.

She reached up to clutch Sawyer's shoulders, and in response, he made a low, growling sound and deepened the kiss.

Her brain radioed the message that she'd been right to steer clear of him in the past. The man was pure testosterone poured into a suit—and he was sending her pheromones into chaos.

Help.

And then the sound of laughter came through the heavy, thick curtains. And just like that, she felt jolted from his sexual spell.

Tearing her lips from Sawyer's, she opened her eyes and shoved him away.

Her heart hammered as he rocked back a half step. But after a moment, his face went smooth and cool.

It was as if the hot lover of a moment ago who had caused her senses to riot had morphed back into the tycoon with an implacable facade.

"Well," Sawyer said slowly, "I guess we answered one question."

A question? She was thinking more in terms of exclamation points. Lots of them.

"Which is?" she huffed.

"We have no problem with sexual chemistry."

Her eyes widened. "Get over yourself."

He gave her a sweeping look, and muttered, "It's you I think I need to get over."

A wave of heat washed over her. An image of Sawyer, naked and looming over her in bed, flashed through her mind.

"You need to come with a warning label!" she shot back.

His smile was rather wolfish. "Isn't that what I'm proposing?" he asked. "Make the world safe for other women. Take me off the market."

"I'm a jewelry designer, not a lion tamer."

"You could be both," he said, his voice smooth as honey.

She cursed herself for finding his sexual banter seductive. Wasn't she an educated, independent woman of the twenty-first century?

Sawyer, on the other hand, was a throwback to feudal

lords—and thanks to his ancestors, he had a real, present-day title to match.

Well, he'd have to look for his countess elsewhere. She didn't know where—though she supposed a fashion event with plenty of beautiful, pedigreed women tottering around in four-inch heels wasn't a half-bad bet—but she knew she wasn't in the running.

"In any case," Sawyer said, breaking into her thoughts, "I'm not proposing what your father has in mind."

"Oh?" she asked with false smoothness. "Then what are you proposing?"

"Your father wants a dynastic marriage. Real but—"

"Loveless," she finished for him before he could spell it out for her.

He nodded. "It's been done for generations."

"This is the twenty-first century."

Of course, it was centuries of ruthless breeding that had produced Sawyer Langsford—a man's man, a captain of industry, a guy who seemed capable of impregnating a woman just by looking at her.

"I'm suggesting a short-term arrangement for our mutual benefit," Sawyer stated.

"A short-term marriage of convenience?" she asked incredulously.

"Right."

"Well, I know what you would get out of the arrangement," she shot back.

"Do you?" he said smoothly.

She ignored the subtext of sexual suggestion. "You'd get control of Kincaid News. But what in the world would be the incentive for me?"

"You'd be doing the right thing for your family," he said, unperturbed. "The majority of your father's media business is in the United Kingdom, while most of my company is in the United States. With corporate synergies, both our companies can continue to prosper. Your father needs a successor for the family firm, and I know the media business."

He added with a quirk of the lips, "Your father would stop trying to interfere in your life. He'd be forever in your debt."

She frowned. "Only because I'd be married to you!"

The price was too high.

"We'd seem to be married for a short while," Sawyer allowed. "But we'd both know the truth."

She felt an unexpected twinge, and then despite herself, she asked, "What about divorce? What happens to the companies then?"

"Once the companies have merged, I'm betting there'll be no turning back. Your father will have his money, and he'll be forced to concede the efficacy of the deal."

"How convenient for you," she responded. "You get your hands on Kincaid holdings without the long-term baggage of a Kincaid bride."

Sawyer's lips quirked again, and this time, she itched to wipe the smile off his face.

"I wouldn't call you a piece of baggage," he said.

"I'm not marrying you."

"There'd be additional benefits for you."

"Those being what?" she retorted.

"I'm in a position to help you move your jewelry business to the next level," he said. "In a way your father hasn't been."

Her spine stiffened. "There are too many strings attached," she said warily. "Anyway, what do you know about my design business?"

"I know Kincaid has refused to become an investor."

Tamara relaxed. It was apparent Sawyer's only clue about her business had come through her father.

She conceded that Sawyer's persistence was a valuable business trait. But she wasn't going to base her married life on a business deal—especially one where she had little to gain and all of her hard-won independence to lose.

"No thanks," she retorted. "I've got the situation well in hand."

"There you are!"

At the sound of a familiar voice, Tamara turned around and discovered Tom making his way toward them along the line of draped curtains, one champagne flute in each hand.

How had Tom thought to look for her here? Still, she was grateful for the rescue.

"Sorry, babe," Tom said. "I was intercepted by someone I knew. He was a guy who used to play some of the same gigs as Zero Sum."

Tom was the quintessential yet-to-make-it-big rocker. He was slightly unkempt, his brown hair curling at the neck of a black T-shirt and matching jacket. He and his band, Zero Sum, hadn't given up on looking for their big break.

Tom had been her occasional date for the past year, whenever he was in town. But right now, Tamara couldn't help contrasting him to Sawyer, who stood about half a head taller, and a world of difference away in smoothness.

Tamara considered herself tall—or at least, not short—at five-seven, but Sawyer had a considerable height advantage on her.

"Tom, you know his lordship, the Earl of Melton, don't you?" she asked, using Sawyer's title in order to strive for some emotional distance between them.

Sawyer's look said he saw right through her ploy.

She ignored him. "My lord, may I present Tom Vance?"

She watched as Sawyer and Tom shook hands and took each other's measure.

"Melton as in Melton Media?" Tom asked.

"One and the same," Sawyer replied.

Tom's face brightened. "Pleasure to meet you, ah—"

"My lord," Tamara supplied, trying not to roll her eyes.

"My lord," Tom repeated, and then shot a grateful look at her. "Thanks, Tam."

"Tam?" Sawyer queried sardonically. "Like Tom and Tam?"

"You've got it." Tom grinned, happy as a puppy.

Tamara could see the wheels turning in Tom's head. To Tom, meeting Sawyer was like hitting the networking jackpot. Sawyer's media outlets presented limitless opportunities. Free publicity! Advertising! Name recognition! In short, the kind of opportunity that Tamara's father refused to provide to Zero Sum.

Sawyer glanced at her. "Tam—Ms. Kincaid, excuse me, won't you? There's someone who's expecting me."

Tamara had no doubt Sawyer had switched from *Tam* to her surname in order to mock her. Still, she was grateful their encounter was at an end.

Unfortunately, she didn't think they'd also put an end to the subject of a dynastic merger—marital, corporate or otherwise.

Three

The bar of the Carlyle Hotel was as good a place as any for three notorious bachelors to lie low.

Or rather, two notorious bachelors and one notorious groom, Sawyer amended.

It was ironic for him to lie low, since he was the press. But these were his friends.

Like his two fellow aristocrats, he'd grown up here, there and everywhere. Still, despite their peripatetic existence, he and his bar companions had managed to become friends.

And now they had another thing in common. Ever since the wedding fiasco at St. Bart's nearly two weeks ago, they were imbrued by the scandal of the moment.

The bar, with its dark woods and mellow lighting, was masculine and clubby and the perfect atmosphere to come together and commiserate.

It was also discreet without being sequestered. Because Sawyer would be damned if he was going to tuck in his tail and hide.

"Hell of way to crash a wedding, Easterbridge," James Carsdale, Duke of Hawkshire, said, going straight to the heart of the matter.

"You could have given us some warning," Sawyer added drily.

Sawyer had to admire Colin's sangfroid. Of the three of them, the marquess was the most reserved and enigmatic. And now he'd just thrown not one, but two ancient British families into upheaval with his surprising news at the wedding—and his shock-maximizing method of delivery.

In response, Colin Granville, Marquess of Easterbridge, who'd been the last to arrive, took a swallow of his Scotch on the rocks.

They were sitting at one corner of the bar, away from the few other patrons. Since it was a hot and sunny day, and still a couple of hours from sunset, the dark bar was not even half-full.

"You're the media, Melton, and you were a groomsman," Colin finally pointed out lazily. "A double conflict of interest. You'll understand why I didn't take you into my confidence."

Sawyer took issue. "You know I was picked as a groomsman because Dillingham and I are distantly related through our mothers. We're not friendly in a true sense."

"Yes," Colin responded wryly, "but that fact, along with your role as one of the world's most famous press barons, made you dynamite for the wedding party. The expectation of glowing press coverage was likely more than Dillingham could pass up. Not to mention cementing the extended family relationship."

Sawyer shook his head. "As it turned out, the only dynamite at the wedding was you, and Dillingham got more media coverage than he bargained for."

In response, Colin raised his glass in mock salute.

"If you couldn't confide in Melton," Hawk said, resting his

elbow on the back of his chair so he could lean back in his position between his companions, "you could've at least told me."

"Spoken like a true international man of mystery, Mr. Fielding," Colin returned.

Sawyer smothered a laugh. He couldn't picture their carefree, sandy-haired friend trying to pass himself off as a mere mister. Nor did he understand why Hawk would have wanted to.

"Right, and what's going on there Hawk?" Sawyer asked. "The rumor mill, and pardon me for reading my own newspapers, has it that you were more than friendly with a certain lovely wedding planner—"

Hawk grimaced. "What's going on is a private matter."

"Precisely my point," Colin said.

"A private matter, Your Grace?" Sawyer quizzed. "You mean between you and your alias, James Fielding?"

"Put a sock in it, Melton," the duke growled.

"Yes, Melton," Colin said, siding with Hawk, "unless you'd like us to quiz you on your pursuit of the fair Ms. Kincaid."

It was Sawyer's turn to grimace. His friends knew his acquisition of Kincaid News was tied up with Tamara's hand in marriage. Fortunately, they *didn't* know the particulars about his most recent interactions with Tamara. She'd gotten under his skin—so much so that he'd kissed her. And it had been some kiss—hot and wonderful enough to leave a man thirsting for more.

"I've seen Kincaid's daughter with a date," Hawk commented, arching a brow. "Always the same one."

Sawyer shrugged. "She takes a date from time to time."

"A date who's not you," Colin pointed out.

"Just an occasional date?" Hawk probed. "And you know this how?"

Sawyer gave a Cheshire-cat grin. "From the man himself,

Mr. Tom Vance, lately of the rock band Zero Sum, and perhaps soon to be the recipient of some very good career news."

Colin quirked an eyebrow, for once betraying a hint of surprise.

Hawk started to shake his head. "Don't go there…"

Since he already had, Sawyer gave both of them a bland look. "Know of any good West Coast record producers?"

She was sunk.

Or more accurately, practically destitute.

Tamara stared at the letter in her hand. Her bid for investors had fallen flat. Financing was tight these days, and people apparently weren't lining up to give money to a lone jewelry designer with a big idea and not much else to her name.

She'd maxed out her credit cards and had already gobbled up her allotment of small business loans.

She looked around her loft from her seat at a workbench cluttered with pliers, clasps and assorted gemstones. Her business had a name, Pink Teddy Designs, and not much else these days. Yesterday, she'd received notice her rent would be increasing, so soon even the four walls around her would cease to exist—as far as she and her business went, anyway.

She'd have to find another place to live and work. There was no way she could afford a ten percent rent increase—not with things the way they were.

She'd never have admitted this to Sawyer when she'd encountered him last week at the fashion party in TriBeCa, but these days she was hanging by a thread—one that was becoming very frayed very fast, ever since she'd left her salaried position two years ago at a top jewelry design firm to strike out on her own.

Rats.

She was desperate—and Sawyer's words reverberated through her mind. *I'm in a position to help you move your jewelry business to the next level.*

No, she wouldn't let herself go there.

And with any luck, Sawyer didn't have a clue as to just how dire her current financial situation was. He hadn't seemed as if he did. In fact, his words to her that night indicated he thought she was looking to expand her business, not merely survive.

She hoped her appearance had also served to throw him off the scent. She'd dressed to project an image of success. She'd worn expensive earrings of her own design to the fashion party—as much for advertising as for anything else, though the earrings were worth much more than the typical Pink Teddy piece of semiprecious jewelry.

Yes, she dreamed of expanding her business and having her name added to the roster of top celebrity jewelry designers. But she'd also had to start small, given her financing, or rather lack thereof. And now she was nearly broke.

People assumed she had money—or at least connections—as the daughter of a millionaire Scottish viscount. In fact, she was entitled to be addressed as the Honourable Tamara Kincaid and not much else. After her parents' divorce when she was seven, she'd gone to reside in the United States with her mother, who had been able to maintain a respectable, but not settled, lifestyle. Instead, thanks to child-support payments, Tamara had been entrusted to the care of a series of babysitters, schools and summer camps while her peripatetic mother had continued to travel and move them within the United States.

Her mother resided in Houston now with husband number three, the owner of a trio of car dealerships, having finally achieved a measure of stability.

Tamara sighed. Partly because of the physical distance, she and her mother weren't very close, but a fringe benefit was that her mother didn't interfere much in her life.

Of course, she could hardly claim the same benefit with

respect to her father, who owned an apartment in New York City.

But unlike her mother, she'd thumbed her nose at her father's money. Because the strings attached had been more than she'd been able to accept. As she'd grown older, her father had made his opinions known, and her artsy tendencies, her penchant for the bohemian and her taste for the unconventional had not gone over well.

Her father's attempts to meddle had, of course, reached their zenith in his crazy plan to marry her off to Sawyer.

Really, that scheme was beyond ridiculous.

Sure, her parents' marriage had been an ill-advised union between an American and a British aristocrat—a still-naive girl from Houston on the one hand, and the young and ambitious heir to a viscountcy on the other. But her starry-eyed mother, who'd imagined herself in love, had been thrilled by the prospect of residing in a British manor house.

In contrast, Tamara prided herself on being a worldly-wise New Yorker. And much as she hated to admit it, she had her father's skeptical nature. She'd inherited her mother's coloring and features, but that's where similarities ended.

She liked her life just fine. She was bohemian with an edge.

A marriage between her and Sawyer Langsford was laughable. They barely spoke the same language, though she had been known to read his paper, *The New York Intelligencer,* and occasionally watch the Mercury News channel.

To Sawyer's credit, Tamara acknowledged, his media outlets didn't stoop to petty sensationalism. And she had to admit he'd built an international media empire from the two British radio stations and the regional newspaper he'd inherited from his father. At thirty-eight, he'd stuffed a lifetime's worth of career accomplishments into a mere fifteen years or so.

At twenty-eight, she was a decade behind Sawyer in experience and worlds away in outlook. Yes, she wanted her design business to float instead of sinking into the great abyss, and yes, she dreamed of becoming successful. But she didn't aspire to the same lofty heights of empire building that her father and Sawyer did.

She'd effectively been abandoned twice by her father—once, in a transatlantic divorce, and then again by Viscount Kincaid's devotion to his media company. She couldn't—wouldn't—risk acquiring a husband who was from the same mold.

It would be beyond foolhardy, notwithstanding the kiss the other night.

Still, the kiss had repeatedly sneaked into her thoughts over the past few days. Sawyer had made her toes curl. And embarrassingly, she'd clearly responded to him.

But she knew why Sawyer had kissed her. He'd been trying to convince her to agree to a marriage of convenience.

If Sawyer thought she was a pushover for his seduction techniques, however, he had another thing coming. So she'd had a brief and primitive response to his air of raw power and sexuality. She was still well past the age of gullibility—of being swayed by a momentary attraction into a relationship with someone who was so very wrong for her.

In contrast, she and Tom were alike. They enjoyed prowling SoHo at night, appreciated the city, and were both artistic. They were friends, first and foremost.

They weren't two people from very different backgrounds united by lust. In other words, to her relief, they were definitely *not* her parents.

As if on cue, her cell phone rang, and it was Tom.

"You'll never guess what's fallen in my lap," Tom said.

"Okay, I give up. What?" she replied.

"I'm flying out to L.A. to meet with a big music producer. He heard one of our demos and is interested in signing the band."

"Tom, that's wonderful!" Tamara exclaimed. "I didn't even know you were in touch with a producer out in L.A."

Tom laughed. "I wasn't. The guy got his hands on the demo from a friend of a friend."

"See, networking works."

Tom gave an exaggerated sigh. "Here's the thing, babe. I'll be gone. Physically, existentially and in every other way."

She picked up on his meaning.

"What?" she said with mock offense. "You'll no longer be available to be my standby date?"

It was easy for her to adopt a lighthearted tone, she realized. Tom had never been more than a casual, occasional date for her—a reliable escort when she had to attend one social function or another. He was nothing more, despite their Tom-and-Tam epithet, and that was the reason she could be happy for him without rancor.

"Afraid not," Tom responded now. "Will you ever forgive me?"

"If I don't, you could always write a song about it," she teased.

Tom laughed. "You're a pal, Tam."

Tom's words summed up their relationship, Tamara acknowledged. It had always been easy and casual. Such a contrast, she thought darkly, from her fraught interactions with—

No, she wouldn't go there.

"It was a lucky break running into your friend the Earl of Melton."

Tamara started guiltily. "He's not my friend."

"Well, friend or acquaintance—"

"And what do you mean it was a lucky break?" she asked, even as she was touched by a feeling of foreboding.

"Well, this music producer has a friend who socializes with the earl. Seems the earl had heard my music—"

She'd just *bet* Sawyer was a fan of Zero Sum.

"—and had talked it up to a friend of his, who passed along the recommendation to his music industry connection."

Tamara felt a wave of heat wash up her face. He didn't... He wouldn't...

And yet, it was all too convenient.

When she found Sawyer, she was going to let him have it, and then some.

For Tom's sake, however, she forced herself to sound cheerful. There was no reason to rain on Tom's parade by imparting her suspicions about how his lucky break was more than mere luck.

Besides, from Tom's perspective, it didn't matter how his intro to a top music producer had come about. The bottom line was that he was getting his chance to hit it big.

"I owe this all to you, Tam," Tom said gratefully. "I don't need to tell you how tough things have been in the music industry lately, so getting someone to take a chance on Zero Sum is a big deal."

If only Tom knew *exactly* what he owed to her, Tamara thought.

"I'll keep my fingers crossed for you," Tamara said. "Blow them away."

"Thanks, babe. You're the best."

When she ended her call with Tom, she set down the phone and stared at it unseeingly, her brows knitting as she contemplated Sawyer's skullduggery.

She'd barely begun to get herself worked up over Sawyer's fiendishness, however, when the intercom sounded.

After she pressed the intercom button by the front door, she jumped as she heard Sawyer's voice.

She took a deep breath. Apparently her confrontation with Sawyer would occur sooner than she'd expected.

"Come on up," she said with a semblance of serenity, and buzzed him in.

Four

Trust Tamara to name her company something ridiculous and suggestive like Pink Teddy Designs, Sawyer thought as he rode the elevator up to the third floor.

The name had been emblazoned next to the buzzer for Tamara's apartment in a cast-iron warehouse building that had long ago been converted into lofts. Located along one of SoHo's narrow side streets, the sidewalk in front of Tamara's building had nevertheless been almost as crowded with pedestrians and street vendors peddling everything from paintings to T-shirts as SoHo's main commercial strips, Broadway and Prince and Spring Streets.

It looked as if Tamara had rented one of the cheaper apartments she could find in one of Manhattan's priciest boho neighborhoods. Factories and warehouses had long since given way to high-end retailers such as Prada, Marc Jacobs and Chanel, though some artists who had bought their lofts when they were cheap still held on.

Of course, Sawyer thought, the businessman in him could

appreciate that Tamara's choice of location made sense. Any business had a certain image to project, and location was part of it. But it seemed as if Tamara had cut corners where she could, starting with choosing a side street and a lower floor, closer to street noises.

He stepped out of the elevator and found Tamara's apartment. But just as he was about to hit the bell, the door opened.

As a first impression, Tamara made quite an impact. In two seconds flat, he registered a short V-neck purple dress, black peep-toe sandals with bows and an opal pendant nestled on the pillow of her cleavage.

His body hummed to life.

"What are you doing here?" Tamara asked, her voice cool and clipped, though her eyes flashed fire.

He twisted his lips sardonically. "That makes twice. Is that the way you greet all your clients?"

"Only the ones who aren't welcome." Then belying her words, she stepped aside. "What do you mean by *client?*"

Sawyer walked into the boxy but airy loft. "I want to have a piece of jewelry designed, if you'll recall."

Tamara's face registered disbelief before her eyes flashed fire again. "You can't be serious."

"That makes twice again. I seem to have a knack for eliciting the same reactions from you." Then he added, in answer to her question, "In fact, I am serious, and I thought you'd be happy about the offer of business."

He watched as she clamped her mouth shut. *Splendid.* He'd stopped her adamancy with a tantalizing lure—a reminder of what he had to offer, and what she stood to lose.

Sawyer scanned the loft. It looked like what his prior investigation had revealed: an apartment that also served as an office and business headquarters.

Near the back, he could see a partition that appeared to section off a sleeping area. To his right, near the entry door, there was a kitchen with light wood cabinets and black appliances. In front of him, the space was dominated by a comfy work area—a deep-red velour couch and armchair, a few potted plants and a large glass-topped table cluttered with what looked, at a glance, like the tools of the jewelry-making trade. A workbench stood off to one side.

The entire space was marked by a high ceiling and accentuated by large, inverted-U-shaped windows that let in plenty of natural light—a precious commodity in Manhattan's pricey real estate market.

Hearing a click as Tamara shut the door behind him, he walked with deliberate casualness to a nearby waist-high glass display case.

He let his eyes scan the bracelets, necklaces and earrings on display, all made from some type of green gemstone.

"It's green agate, in case you're wondering," Tamara said crisply as she stopped beside him.

He looked up from the case, and she regarded him challengingly, almost defensively.

"I was reading your stare," she explained.

"You have a unique style."

"Thank you, I think."

His lips quirked up. "You're welcome."

She looked pointedly at his custom-made business suit, as if making a silent judgment about the contrast in their two styles.

Perhaps she was also wondering why he'd bothered to fit a visit with her into his busy work schedule.

He wasn't about to accommodate her unspoken question, however. Because the truth was, though it was late Wednesday afternoon and the middle of his workweek, he'd cleared his schedule in order to come downtown and find her. And if Tamara knew the importance he'd attached to his visit, she'd clam up and retreat. Or more likely, it would raise her hackles again.

"What sort of commission do you have in mind?" she asked finally, saving him from a response.

He figured it was too much to hope she'd had an abrupt change of heart about creating jewelry for him. More likely, her curiosity was simply piqued. But he'd work with that for now.

"A coordinated set," he said blandly. "Earrings and a necklace."

"Of course," she responded with a corresponding lack of inflection. "Do you prefer a particular type of stone?"

He looked into her eyes. "Emeralds."

"A popular choice—" she gave him a saccharine smile "—but I can't help you. I focus on bridge jewelry made with semiprecious stones—"

"Designing fine jewelry with precious stones can't be much different," he countered.

Tamara hesitated before conceding grudgingly, "No, it's not."

"Great, then there's no problem," he responded smoothly. "Which stones do you like?"

She frowned. "I don't see how that enters—"

"You're a professional designer," he diverted. "I'd like to know what you think. What stones do you prefer, assuming money isn't an issue?"

She clenched her jaw. "Emeralds. Dark-toned ones."

He gave a satisfied smile. "Then we're in agreement. Make them big, and surrounded by diamonds."

She pursed her lips. "Has it ever occurred to you that I simply might not like a commission from you?"

"Never." He flashed a smile. "You're in business to sell jewelry, and I'm here prepared to spend six figures."

With an oblique reference, he cast another lure for her. He was a seasoned player at the negotiation table and now he brought his skills to bear.

She looked exasperated. "You are decisive."

"Yes, I am." He hid his satisfaction in the chink in her armor. "Aren't most of your clients?"

"I don't usually do custom orders," she responded. "It's not how I operate. The people who buy my jewelry appreciate something offbeat."

He grinned. "Not your usual high-society bling bling."

At her nod, he added, "Then I hope you can…accommodate me."

It was sexual banter, but he was careful to keep his expression innocent. Nevertheless, she regarded him with suspicious displeasure for a moment.

"No request is too unusual," she replied finally.

"What a relief."

She raised her eyebrows. "I'll need a deposit, and you'll have to give me time to contact my suppliers and find the right stones. Fat emeralds are not among my usual orders."

Touché. Still, he was happy to have her think of him as gaudy and tasteless as long as it got him one step closer to his goal. "Naturally, I understand. I hope I'm not putting you out."

"Not any more than the unexpected appearance of a persistent would-be client," she shot back.

The shadow of a smile touched his lips. Tamara certainly knew how to give as good as she got. What a waste she would have been on Tom. Sawyer was not the least bit repentant about his ruthless maneuvering.

Rather than respond directly to her jab, he turned the conversation in the direction he wanted it to go. "I thought you'd be happy about an expensive order." He glanced around at their surroundings. "I understand you could use some help."

Now that he had her on the hook, he could afford to drive his point home.

Tamara hesitated. "What makes you think so?"

"I have my sources."

She scowled suddenly. "Have you been talking to my father?" She held up a hand, as if to stop him. "No, wait. Don't bother answering that question."

"For the record, it was through my own digging. But what I didn't find out on my own, your friend Tom was happy to volunteer."

She ignored the reference to Tom and braced one hand on her hip, her eyes narrowing. "You had me investigated?"

He let his lips quirk up on one side. "I like to know who I'm doing business with. Avoids nasty surprises."

"So I should be flattered?" she demanded, looking outraged. "Is it a compliment that I merited the same full-blown investigation you might accord to a prospective business partner?"

"In or out of bed," he added to get a rise out of her.

Her face flushed with color. "I see." She gave him a sweeping look. "And I suppose none of your…girlfriends were infuriated by having to pass muster? Was the privilege of sleeping with you just too great a prize?"

He gave her a slow grin designed to incense. "No complaints yet."

"Oh!"

For a moment, she looked as if she was speechless with outrage, fishing around for the right words for a proverbial clobbering.

Finally, she bit out, "I suppose that's why you're here today—to order a trinket for one of the lucky winners?"

He cocked his head to the side, and then raised his hand to slowly brush a tendril back from her face.

She stilled.

"You could characterize it that way," he said in a deep voice that held just a hint of laughter.

She brushed his hand aside. "Fine," she huffed, her voice nonetheless holding a hint of breathlessness. "It's not my business why my clients come to me—or how."

"Not too discriminating to do business with the devil?" he baited her.

She gave him a narrow-eyed look. "Let's step over to my desk to discuss what you're looking for." She paused, and then added emphatically, almost warningly, "In a necklace and earrings coordinate set, of course."

He gave a low laugh as he followed her.

This sale was costing her, but she was gritting her teeth and bearing it since she needed the money. Pink Teddy Designs meant a great deal to her, and he planned to exploit the attachment to his every advantage.

Shamelessly...ruthlessly...unrepentantly.

Because if there was one thing he knew, Sawyer acknowledged as he admired Tamara's backside and shapely legs, it was that Kincaid News was worth the effort...and so was Tamara. And certainly, it would be no hardship to bed Tamara along the way to getting what he wanted.

At her desk—which was actually the large, glass-topped table he'd seen earlier—he sat in a bar-height chair at a right angle to her.

"So describe to me what you're looking for." She set aside some metal boxes so they sat out of her way, and added belatedly, "In earrings and a necklace."

"In earrings and a necklace, of course," he murmured, echoing her words.

In fact, he'd love to describe what he was looking for—in and out of bed.

The truth was, he acknowledged to himself with some degree of surprise, if he'd ever let himself really look over the years, he'd have said Tamara wasn't too far off the mark from what he usually looked for in a woman, though he'd never dated a redhead.

She had inherited her mother's model looks and figure. She had generous breasts and hips, but still managed to look willowy and statuesque. And she had amazing bone structure.

Her lips were full, balanced by an aquiline nose and delicately arched brows over crystalline green eyes. She was good enough to grace the cover of any glamour magazine, if she chose. That she *didn't* choose said a lot about her.

Physically, she fit his type. But he'd always envisioned someone who embraced his aristocratic heritage as his bride.

Tamara pulled a white paper pad in front of her, and then reached for a pencil. "Describe to me what you're looking for. If the design isn't to your liking, we can always play around with it. Computerized design technology is an amazing thing these days, but I prefer to start with an old-fashioned sketch."

He cocked his head and regarded her. "Something unique. Something that will have people take a second look."

"That's a wide universe," she replied archly, her pencil hovering.

He shrugged. "Let your imagination run wild."

She gave him another narrow-eyed look, as if she was thinking of hitting him over the head, or wondering at his audacity—the equivalent of asking the wife to pick out a gift for the mistress.

"I'm thinking of a choker," she said sweetly.

He laughed softly, and she put down her pencil and reached for a three-ring binder.

"Here," she said. "These might give you some ideas. They're some computerized drawings I've done."

"Great," he said, taking the binder from her.

While he paged through her drawings, she occupied herself with arranging objects on her desk and pointedly ignoring his study of her designs.

Finally, he set the binder on the table with deliberate casualness. He wasn't going to let her off the hook too easily. He knew what he wanted, and he wasn't going to stop until he got it.

"These are good, but I need more," he said.

She looked nonplussed. "More?"

"Yes. It would be better if you modeled some of your designs for me."

It took a moment for his words to sink in, but then her eyes flared, and their gazes clashed.

He shrugged, a smile playing at his lips. "Call it a singular lack of imagination."

He watched as she seemed to grit her teeth. How much was she willing to do for a lucrative commission?

He could practically see the wheels turning in her head. How far would she go to indulge his whims?

"Which one?" she finally asked with exaggerated patience.

He had little doubt her use of the singular was deliberate. She had no intention of modeling any more than the bare minimum for him.

Ignoring her hint of impatience, he picked up the binder again and thumbed through it.

Her designs were good. Better than good. He'd inherited the Langsford family jewels, and in addition, he'd bought his share of pricey jewelry over the years, so he was no novice buyer. And to his practiced eye, these designs looked fresh and different.

"This one," he said, stopping at a page and showing it to her.

She shook her head. "That piece has been sold. I don't have another one here like it."

Unperturbed, he moved on to another page. "What about this one?"

"That's topaz. The yellow gold setting wouldn't be right for diamonds and emer—"

"Humor me," he said with all the assurance of someone used to calling the shots—and being right. "I'm not looking at the metal but at the design."

"Right. Of course."

He hid a smile. *The client was always right.* She couldn't argue there, much as she obviously wanted to.

Tamara pushed back her chair and marched over to a safe across the width of the loft. After opening the safe door, she removed two velvet boxes.

Sawyer watched her intently, his body stirring.

Without looking at him, she stepped over to the gilded full-length mirror mounted on the nearby wall.

From the smaller of the two boxes, she retrieved one earring and then another, putting them on one by one.

Sawyer shifted in his chair.

"You need to put your hair up in order to show them off properly," he said, his voice resonating in the quiet room.

Tamara compressed her lips, but then, with a show of impatience, as if she found all this ridiculous, and still refusing to look at him, she reached into a nearby drawer. She removed a plastic clip, and proceeded to put up her hair.

Sawyer parted his lips and sucked in a deep breath as heat shot through him.

The image in the mirror was enticing, enchanting even. When was the last time he'd seen Tamara with her hair up?

The earrings were about two inches long, the large, multifaceted topaz stones at the ends of them catching the light. They moved fluidly along with Tamara, brushing the tendrils of hair that had failed to find a home in her plastic clip.

Sawyer resisted the urge to go to her and press his lips to the tender curve of her neck. He knew he was playing a dangerous game that he was at risk of getting caught up in himself.

Tamara bent to the larger of the two velvet boxes and lifted out an exquisite and elaborate fringelike necklace with topaz stones.

Sawyer stood up abruptly. "Let me help you."

Before she could argue, he was behind her, taking the necklace from her unresisting fingers.

"I'm an expert at doing and undoing clasps," she protested weakly.

"Nevertheless, let me make the gallant gesture."

"Practicing for the real moment?" Tamara tossed out, her words belying her response of sexual awareness, her nipples outlined against the fabric of her dress.

Sawyer let his lips curve lazily. "If I were, then I'd do this next."

He didn't think. He just gave in to temptation.

Fortunately, in this case, business and pleasure were one and the same.

Five

Tamara felt a sizzle shoot through her as Sawyer nuzzled her ear, and then bit down gently on her earlobe, the large topaz stone of her earring rocking between them as he did so.

She swallowed, holding back a small gasp. Sawyer's body, hard and unyielding, brushed against hers, igniting a simmering heat in her.

Tamara was mesmerized by their image in the mirror.

Sawyer toyed with the delicate shell of her ear, and then his mouth closed over her earlobe again and gave a gentle tug. All the while, his breath sent small shivers coursing through her.

Tamara closed her eyes. It was her only defense. The image in the mirror was just too erotic.

Sawyer's hands gently kneaded her shoulders.

"Relax," he said in a low voice.

Tamara struggled against the undertow of his seduction. She already knew the power of his kiss, and a part of her couldn't believe she'd allowed him to get this close—again. What had she been thinking?

She'd reached with greedy hands when he'd offered the enticement of a hefty sale. His down payment alone would be enough to cover her monthly rent. But then what?

This was the road to ruin.

"Sawyer..."

But before she could say more, he turned her to face him, and his mouth came down on hers.

His lips were warm and supple, and he deepened the kiss before she had time to marshal her forces.

The kiss washed over her like a warm summer rain, making her feel vital and alive. In her head, she was spinning, her head thrown back with laughter, her nipples plastered to her wet clothes.

Sawyer kissed the way he did everything—confidently, decisively...persuasively. And more importantly, the effect of his kiss on her was powerful and shocking.

His hips pressed against her, making her want to rub against him. With very little effort, he had her restless and aroused.

The kiss that Sawyer had stolen at the fashion party *hadn't* been a fluke. And wasn't that the real explanation for why she'd let things progress to this point? Because the question had been dogging her?

He was in the wrong field, she thought absently. He should be hawking kisses instead of news. Then he'd be even richer than he was.

Sawyer's arms, all hard muscle, banded around her, and one hand settled on her backside, molding their bodies together. Her arms crept around his neck, drawing him to her. She wiggled closer, brushing against his arousal and eliciting a throaty growl from Sawyer.

Tamara knew if she was honest with herself, she'd admit she'd never experienced a kiss like Sawyer's. But then forbidden fruit was a powerful aphrodisiac.

Still, a shred of reason intervened. *This was her last chance.*

With a last bit of resolve, she tore her mouth from his. "Wait a minute!"

She flattened her hand on his chest, but the steady, strong beat of his heart, his warmth and solidity, seemed to brand her, and she snatched back her hand.

Sawyer's eyes glittered with golden fire.

Summoning a determination she didn't feel, Tamara opened her mouth.

"Don't lie to yourself, and don't lie to me," Sawyer said softly, his tone nevertheless conveying a note of implacability.

Her brows snapped together. Well, she wasn't going to engage in any hollow denials. But she didn't like the way he'd thrown her off balance.

"What do you want?" she said.

"I think you already know."

"You came in here for a necklace," she persisted.

"Among other things."

How could he seem so rational when she was still trying to recover from the effect of their kiss?

"Don't think you can seduce me into changing my mind about your proposal."

"Fine," he said, gimlet-eyed. "But I'm offering a way for you to save Pink Teddy Designs. I thought that would appeal to the small-business owner in you."

She hated that he knew what straits she was in. She hated that he had well-honed instincts and knew her weak spots.

"I see," she said coolly, striving to match her tone to his. "I suppose if you're going to torpedo my social life, you feel you owe it to me to at least help me professionally?"

He arched a brow. "Are you talking about Tom?"

"Yes!"

"There was no passion there."

"How do you know?" she retorted.

"The cutesy moniker says it all. 'Tam and Tom.' You sounded like pals."

"Meaning you'd never be caught dead dating someone who was worthy of a cutesy little tandem name?"

"Correct," he said, and then added bluntly, "Did you sleep with him?"

A note of belligerence had entered his tone. She knew Sawyer's purpose was to dismiss Tom as inconsequential.

"It's none of your business," she snapped.

"I'll take that as a no," Sawyer said. "Poor bastard. I thought so."

She wanted to wipe the satisfied expression off his face. "Tom is one of the good guys. He isn't after control of my father's company."

"Don't kid yourself, sweetheart. Tom isn't a saint." Sawyer's eyes swept over her. "On the other hand, since he kept his hands off of you, maybe he is."

Tamara felt a strange thrill. Had Sawyer just admitted to finding her hard to resist?

She pushed the question away. She reminded herself that Sawyer was simply trying to get his way. He'd say or do *anything* to sway her. He was ruthless. Just like her father.

With that thought, she scoffed, "What could you possibly have to pin on Tom?"

Sawyer looked her in the eye. "Maybe he was dating you because of your connection to Kincaid News."

Her eyes widened. "You're despicable!"

"He jumped at the opportunity to go to L.A., didn't he?"

"Only because you arranged to make him an irresistible offer!"

Tamara reluctantly recalled that Tom had asked her about Kincaid News, even after she'd explained to him that help was unlikely to come for his band from that quarter. Still, she refused to see his interest in her as less than genuine.

"He was quick to sell you out with information about your current financial situation," Sawyer pointed out ruthlessly. "When it became clear how I could help his career, he was eager as a puppy."

"And you're a puppy in need of obedience training!"

Sawyer's lips quirked with amusement. "Volunteering for the job?"

"No, thank you."

Sawyer's expression became enigmatic. "At least I've been clear about what I want."

"Yes," she retorted disdainfully. "Kincaid News."

"No, you and Kincaid News," he contradicted, and then his look softened. "I'm offering you a final chance to salvage your dream. Isn't becoming a jewelry designer what you've always wanted to do?"

She was like Eve being tempted by the apple, Tamara thought. How had he known she'd always wanted to be a designer? Even though she knew it was part of his persuasive ploy, it was refreshing to have someone at least pretend to take her dream seriously.

"I remember visiting Dunnyhead once," he mused, naming her father's estate in Scotland. "You were wearing a bead bracelet that you'd made yourself."

Tamara was surprised Sawyer remembered. Her father had given her a jewelry-making kit during her stay at Dunnyhead. She'd just turned twelve, and it had been one of the few times after her parents' divorce her father had seemed aware of her interests and hobbies.

She'd strung together translucent green beads from the kit into a fair semblance of a hippie bracelet. Her father, she recalled, hadn't been particularly impressed. Still, she'd kept her beaded creation for years afterward.

During that stay at Dunnyhead, she recalled she'd played with her younger sisters, Julia and Arabella, who'd been five and two. But until this moment, she hadn't remembered Sawyer's visit.

"Who did you want to be when you grew up?" Sawyer probed, his tone inviting. "You must have had someone you aspired to be like."

"I wanted to be an original," she replied, her defenses lowering a notch.

Sawyer gave a low laugh. "Of course. I should have guessed. Tamara Kincaid has always been unique."

Despite herself, a smile of shared amusement rose to her lips. "After the divorce," she divulged, "my mother kept some pieces from Bulgari, Cartier and Harry Winston that my father had given her."

"And I bet you loved putting them on," he guessed.

"My father wouldn't let me play in the family vault," she deadpanned.

"I'd let you play with the Melton jewels," he joked, but his eyes gleamed like polished stones. "Hell, you could wear them to your heart's content."

"Trying to bribe me?" she said lightly.

"Whatever works."

Her eyes came to rest beyond Sawyer. She saw her workbench scattered with the implements of a jeweler's trade.

All of it, however, was in danger of disappearing from her life. And suddenly, inexplicably, what Sawyer offered was so very tempting.

Would it be so bad?

"It wouldn't be terrible," he said, as if reading her mind. "A short-term marriage of convenience gets us what we both want, and then we go our separate ways."

"As opposed to my father's proposal of a real but bloodless and indefinite dynastic marriage?"

Sawyer inclined his head.

"You're proposing that we double-cross my father?"

"I wouldn't put it that way," Sawyer replied, "but one rascal deserves another, don't you think?"

The image that his words conjured brought an involuntary smile to her lips. Would it matter to her father what type of marriage she and Sawyer contracted if the bottom line was that he got what he wanted—seeing Kincaid News into capable hands?

And yet. "We'll never convince my father that we have a real marriage."

Sawyer arched a brow. "We've just proven we'll have no problem convincing people the passion is real."

She felt a rippling warmth suffuse her.

When had she turned so hot and bothered where Sawyer was concerned? Perhaps when she'd discovered their kisses had her seeing a kaleidoscope of colors.

Still, she hedged. "You said this would be a marriage of convenience."

He gave her a bland look. "Are you asking whether I'd expect you to share my bed?"

She kept her expression unchanged, but at her sides, her fingers curled into her palms. "I just want us to be clear."

He smiled lazily. "The answer is no. That is, unless you decide you'd like to be in my bed."

"Hardly," she replied tartly.

His eyes laughed at her. "A man can dream."

She felt a quiver in response to his compelling magnetism. She turned away to hide her reaction, surveying her domain, and then hugging herself. What was she willing to give up to save this?

Not too discriminating to do business with the devil.

Sawyer's words came back to her, and now she knew he was right.

"Six months," she said without looking at him. "That should be more than enough time—"

"However long it takes."

"You said it would be short-term," she countered, her tone faintly accusatory.

He settled his hands on her shoulders, warm and caressing. "I'm looking forward to it."

When he bent and nuzzled her neck, she closed her eyes. He kissed her throat, and she couldn't help thinking he was sealing the deal.

And then a moment later, he was gone, out the door.

With her fingertips, she touched the still warm and tingly spot where he'd kissed her.

What had she done by bargaining with the devil?

"I'm going to marry Sawyer Langsford."

Her statement was met with a joint gasp.

Tamara looked from one to the other of her friends. Pia's eyes had gone wide, while Belinda just looked at her in frozen silence, her coffee cup halfway to her lips.

They were sitting in Contadini having a casual Sunday brunch, but her announcement blew the relaxed atmosphere right out of the water.

Tamara glanced at Pia. "Any chance you can squeeze a small and hasty English wedding into your schedule for next month?"

"Oh, dear Lord," Belinda breathed, rolling her eyes. "Tell me you're not pregnant!"

Tamara looked at her friend in alarm. "Of course not!"

Was it her use of the word *hasty* that had made Belinda jump straight to pregnancy?

Belinda set down her cup. "Well, we can rule out drunk, since it's Sunday morning and you're sipping orange juice, so...what is going on?"

"She looks sane to me," Pia murmured to Belinda, who nodded in agreement.

Belinda and Pia were both back in New York for the moment, and Tamara had decided that now, at one of their regular brunches, was as good a time as any to spring her momentous news on them.

"Of course I haven't lost my mind," she said.

At least, she didn't think she had.

Belinda gave her a penetrating look. "Has your father strong-armed you into this? I know he saw you and Sawyer together at the wedding reception—"

"Oh, Tamara," Pia jumped in, her brow puckered, "there has to be a way out!"

"And it's easier to find a way out before the wedding than after," Belinda muttered.

Tamara took a fortifying breath. "My father hasn't pressed anything." *Sort of.* If it hadn't been for her father's conditions on the merger of Kincaid News with Melton Media, Sawyer would never have proposed. It was a humiliating way to have received her first marriage proposal, but a humiliation that brought salvation for her business. "In fact, I've hardly ever given a decision this much calculated thinking."

"Uh-oh," Pia breathed. "Calculated thinking for a wedding? Oh, Tamara!"

Tamara repressed a sigh. Of course, Pia, the eternal romantic, would be shocked and alarmed at the idea of a marriage of convenience.

"Beats the opposite," Belinda put in. "I don't recommend the impetuous elopement."

Tamara raised her hand. "Hear me out."

"I'm all ears," Belinda replied. "This I have to hear."

Tamara steadied herself. "You both know Pink Teddy Designs has been in financial difficulty for some time." It was a painful admission. Her business was everything to her—her dream, her quest for validation. "But what you don't know is that recently things have come to a head. My rent is set to increase and I've tapped out my credit."

Belinda's eyes narrowed. "So you're marrying Sawyer for financial reasons?" she guessed. "Can I just weigh in with the fact that money is on my list of bad reasons to get married?"

Pia shook her head. "It'll never last."

Tamara pushed at her breakfast plate. "I don't want it to last!"

Pia's eyes rounded. "And what about poor Tom?"

"Poor Tom is on his way to Los Angeles, hot on the trail of a record deal, thanks to Sawyer."

"Wonderful," Belinda remarked sarcastically.

"I mentioned my father had a long-cherished wish to unite the Kincaid and Langsford families," Tamara said. "But what I didn't mention is that he's made his agreement to Melton Media's merger with Kincaid News conditional on Sawyer convincing me to marry him."

Pia gasped, her hand briefly covering her mouth. "You're willing to throw away your chance to marry for love?"

Tamara was tempted to say she was a bit cynical about love after the examples set by her parents, but she stifled her reply. She supposed in Pia's business, it was helpful—maybe even necessary—to believe in true love. Why disabuse her friend?

And, truth be told, Tamara conceded, she wasn't a *hardened* cynic. Her secret indulgence was chick flicks that made her misty-eyed. She'd wonder whether it was possible to find a man who set her pulse racing *and* held her close to his heart. She'd wonder if, despite her parents' example, a happily-ever-after was attainable for her.

She pasted a smile on her face. "No, don't worry. I'm not giving up the chance of love forever. With any luck—" her lips twisted self-deprecatingly "—a second marriage will be the charm."

"Or third," Belinda muttered.

"Or third," she agreed, since it was clear her friend was hoping for a third wedding.

Thrusting aside the fact that her own father had been

married three times, Tamara quickly explained the terms of her agreement with Sawyer for a short-term marriage of convenience: Kincaid News in return for the money to save Pink Teddy Designs.

"I don't know," Pia said doubtfully when she'd finished, shaking her head.

"What could go wrong?" Tamara asked. "In six months, a year at most, we both go our separate ways."

"Famous last words," Belinda said. "It's taken me more than two years to get an annulment."

Tamara needed to know her friends were behind her. More importantly, she needed both her friends' help if she was to convince her father that she and Sawyer had succumbed to dynastic expectations rather than come up with a plan of their own.

"I need you both to act as if you believe Sawyer and I have finally decided to do our family duty," she said baldly. "Otherwise I'll never convince my father."

Pia's eyes widened, and Belinda snorted disbelievingly.

"Your father will never buy it," Belinda said.

"It's my only hope."

Her only hope, and Pink Teddy's.

Neither Belinda nor Pia had a ready reply, but Tamara could tell from their expressions that they reluctantly understood her predicament.

She sucked in a breath. "So will you do it? Will you show up when I marry—" she stumbled over the word, and Belinda looked at her keenly "—Sawyer? Even if it turns out to be in a drafty British castle?"

Belinda sighed. "I'll bring my Wellingtons."

"And I'll help coordinate," Pia chimed in.

Tamara glanced from one to the other of her friends. "Even if Colin and Hawk are almost certainly going to be there at Sawyer's invitation?"

There was a palpable pause.

Pia grimaced. "You know you can count on me. Just keep me away from the hors d'oeuvres."

"I'll bring my attorney," Belinda added grimly.

Tamara laughed.

For a moment, thanks to her friends, she could forget just how complicated a situation she was getting into.

Still, this was surely going to be some wedding.

Six

"Tell him to come in," Sawyer said into the speakerphone, and then rose from behind his desk.

Floor-to-ceiling windows revealed a spectacular view of the Hudson River. The corporate offices of Melton Media were located on the upper floors of a gleaming midtown Manhattan building.

Sawyer had taken several strides when his office door opened and Viscount Kincaid strolled in.

"Melton," the viscount acknowledged jovially as he came forward and shook hands.

Sawyer wasn't fooled for a second. Though Tamara's father was a couple of inches shorter than his own six-two, the older man had an air of prepossession and command that only someone born into authority or accustomed to it for a long time could exude.

In Kincaid, diabolically, the genial visage of a Santa Claus was joined to the shrewd mind of a Machiavelli—a trap for the unwary.

"Shall we proceed down to the executive dining room?" Sawyer asked.

It was well before the daily news deadline for East Coast newspapers going to press, but they were both busy men.

"I'm ready whenever you are," Kincaid said, nevertheless reaching into the inner pocket of his suit jacket for his buzzing BlackBerry.

Kincaid kept up his end of the phone conversation as they made their way downstairs via the suspended metal staircase that joined the executive floors of Melton Media. They were far from the chaos of the newsroom. Melton Media's corporate offices were housed in a separate building from *The New York Intelligencer.*

Sawyer listened as, apparently, Kincaid attempted to verify by phone a juicy rumor that he'd heard at a cocktail party the night before. Clearly, the viscount had the news business in his blood and wasn't averse to rolling up his sleeves and working the phones himself when necessary.

Tellingly, though, Sawyer couldn't discern from Kincaid's end of the conversation what the rumor was or whom the older man was talking to. Sawyer felt the competitive juices start to flow in his blood.

Kincaid was a worthy adversary and would be a worthy business partner.

"Rumor confirmed?" Sawyer asked with feigned idle curiosity when the viscount finished his call.

"Yes," Kincaid replied with a note of satisfaction.

"I thought we were on the same team," Sawyer said with mock reproof.

"Not yet. Not until the merger goes through."

Sawyer's chuckle held an element of respect. Viscount Kincaid might be a family friend, but he was a fierce competitor.

When Sawyer had asked for this meeting, he'd suggested he pay a call to Kincaid headquarters, but the viscount had gainsaid him. Perhaps Kincaid wanted another opportunity to take a look around the company that would soon merge with Kincaid News.

Sawyer had inherited an already significant company from his father and had built it up, branching out internationally from the British newspapers and radio station that his father and grandfather had run. His grandfather had married into the newspaper business by wedding a publishing heiress, but he'd taken to it like a natural.

Kincaid was a different animal altogether. He'd labored in the trenches of the news business, selling family real estate in Scotland to build up his company. His gamble had paid off handsomely, but Kincaid was no fool. He knew that, in order to survive, Kincaid News needed fresh blood—someone well positioned and savvy enough to take advantage of the new mediums of communication out there, from online sites and streaming to smartphones.

Namely, the viscount needed Sawyer.

And Sawyer was eager to absorb a competitor at a relative bargain.

At that thought, Sawyer paused and mentally grimaced. Correction: a relative bargain and a bargaining relative. Kincaid had turned the business into a family legacy, and he wasn't going to let it pass into other hands without a familial tie.

He and the viscount entered the executive dining room, which was one floor below Sawyer's office and had an equally impressive view of the Hudson. The long table had been set for two.

They dined on steak frites accompanied by iced tea. The conversation moved idly from politics and the upcoming elections to the doings of various business associates, until, finally, Viscount Kincaid set aside his fork and fixed Sawyer with a piercing look.

"Well, I know you didn't invite me here to discuss golf," Kincaid said gruffly, "so out with it, Melton."

Unperturbed, Sawyer took his time wiping his mouth and setting aside his napkin. Then he looked at the other man squarely.

"I'd like to ask for Tamara's hand in marriage."

Kincaid's eyebrows rose. "Bloody hell, you've done it."

Sawyer nodded.

"How?"

Sawyer gave a ghost of a smile. "I don't suppose it could be my charm and persuasiveness."

Kincaid shook his head. "Hogwash. Tamara would never fall for it."

"I have been wooing her." It wasn't far from the truth. He *had* been trying to convince Tamara to see things his way.

Kincaid's eyebrows drew together. "Since when?"

"We preferred to conduct our relationship away from prying eyes."

Sawyer thought back to his last private encounter with Tamara. She'd been so responsive in his arms, her luscious female curves pressed into him. And he—he'd wanted to tumble her backward and have hot, sweaty sex with her right there in her studio, her red hair fanning out on that damnable red velour couch.

Sawyer felt his body tighten at the memory, and shifted in his seat. "I think you'll find that Tamara isn't unaware of her familial obligations."

His last statement was met with a pause, but then Kincaid waved it away with one hand. "Certainly not in character," the viscount growled. "She's shown nothing but disregard until now." Kincaid shook his head. "Her sisters, too. Three daughters and not a one with an appreciation of what it took to built Kincaid News or how I footed the bill for those fine prep school educations."

"She does bear you some affection, you know."

Sawyer would bet that beneath Tamara's tartness and Viscount Kincaid's bluster lay a genuine—if oftentimes fraught—bond between father and daughter.

A light appeared in Viscount Kincaid's eyes, but it was quickly replaced by a look of cloaked cunning. "Is that so? Then I'll expect a grandchild to be in the cards in the not too distant future."

Sawyer schooled his expression—this was a complication that he hadn't foreseen. "Perhaps Tamara and I would like to enjoy ourselves first."

"Enjoy yourselves later." Kincaid settled back in his chair. "In fact, I like the idea of a grandchild so much I fancy I'll make it a condition of the merger."

Cagey bastard.

"My daughter *enceinte* before the merger goes through."

"That wasn't part of the agreement."

"How much do you want this merger?"

"As much as you do, I would have thought," Sawyer replied drily.

"I can wait," Kincaid returned. "I've got some life in me yet, and God knows I've long since pinned my hopes on a third generation taking over the reins of Kincaid News." Kincaid leaned forward. "The question is, will you or someone else be a worthy caretaker for Kincaid News in the meantime?"

Sawyer said nothing. He'd learned long ago that a tough bargainer didn't jump in with his next best offer right away. He stayed cool and deliberated his options.

In this case, he supposed he could call the older man's bluff. *Good luck convincing Tamara or either of her sisters to marry another newsman.*

But an image suddenly flashed through his mind of Tamara being bedded by some faceless pretender to the throne of Kincaid News, attempting to conceive the sought-for grandchild. He discovered that the thought of some other man fathering Tamara's child didn't sit well with him.

Better me than some faceless bastard, Sawyer thought.

Kincaid sat back in his seat, a smile hovering at his lips, seemingly satisfied by Sawyer's reaction, or at least lack of immediate objection. "Marrying Tamara is the first step. I'll do everything in my power to see that you actually make it to the altar, including making all the necessary public pronouncements that I'm overjoyed."

"Naturally," Sawyer said sardonically.

Kincaid leaned forward again, apparently warming to his subject. "I've done all I can up till now to help you, including—" Kincaid looked suddenly sly "—sharing all I know about Tamara's comings and goings."

Sawyer had to admit Kincaid had been helpful in that respect. Without inside knowledge, he'd have had a harder time.

"But the second step, the necessary step before I sign over Kincaid News, is getting Tamara pregnant," Kincaid went on, quirking a brow. "And for that, you're on your own."

"Of course," Sawyer said drily.

Kincaid couldn't have put it more baldly. Sawyer would have to entice Tamara into his bed.

"Naturally," Kincaid said, "I won't breathe a word to Tamara about this new condition to the merger."

"Thanks for the small favor."

Kincaid chuckled. "I wouldn't want her to lock you out of the bedroom just out of spite."

"Thwarting you has been a favorite pastime of hers," Sawyer observed with a jab.

The viscount's face darkened briefly. "Yes, but those days are past now…as long as you get her to the altar."

Kincaid's new condition on the merger presented a complication that Sawyer hadn't anticipated. He'd bargained with Tamara for a marriage of short duration. Once they both got what they wanted, they could go their separate ways. A baby had never been part of the equation.

He wasn't thrilled at the prospect of having a child with a divorce envisioned in the future. But then again, he was thirty-eight, his life was destined to become only busier after the business merger with Kincaid News, and he had a duty to the earldom to produce an heir. Sure, he could wait for a woman suitable for the duties of a countess, but right now that prospect seemed highly indeterminate.

On the other side, there was the very concrete reality of *Tamara,* who, however unsuited and averse she might be to being a countess, made his blood sizzle.

His body tightened as images flashed through his mind of just how pleasurable it could be to try to conceive an heir with Tamara.

"So, do you agree to the terms?"

Viscount Kincaid's voice brought Sawyer back from his mental calculations.

Sawyer knew without hesitation what his answer was. "Yes." He reached for his glass and raised it in mock salute. "To the merger of the Kincaid and Melton lines, corporate and otherwise."

Tamara waltzed into Balthazar at noon. It had been an easy walk from her loft. She'd been surprised when Sawyer had called and proposed that they meet at a restaurant in her area.

Now, inside the restaurant entrance, she spotted Sawyer immediately. He looked impeccable, as always, in a red tie and pinstripe suit, even if his hair was a little tousled from the wind outside.

Unconsciously, she smoothed her own hair as he approached her.

"You look fine," he said, his deep voice flowing over her like warm honey.

When she stopped in midmovement, Sawyer's mouth lifted.

"More than fine," he amended. "You look great."

The frank male appreciation that suddenly fired his gaze sent sexual awareness washing over her.

"You don't look too shabby yourself," she responded, surprised at the hint of breathlessness that crept into her voice.

She'd tried not to care when dressing this morning, but she'd given up and finally settled on a short-sleeved heather-gray sweater dress cinched by a thin purple belt and paired with magenta patent platform heels.

She was a rebel with a cause, she'd thought defiantly. She didn't care what a countess was supposed to look like. This is what she looked like.

Sawyer clasped her hand and brushed his lips across hers.

At her surprised reaction, he murmured, "We have to make it look good in public."

Of course. She steadied herself. "I'm surprised you came downtown. I'd have thought Michael's or 21 was more your taste."

Michael's was favored by the media crowd, and 21 was a clubby bastion famous for the jockey figures that adorned its facade.

"I was looking for a place that was a little off the beaten trail," Sawyer returned equably, and then winked. "And I thought I'd show you I can be flexible."

"Well, don't expect me to convene at La Grenouille with the ladies who lunch."

"Perish the thought," he said with mock solemnity, and then smiled. "But I'll turn you into an uptown girl yet."

"That's what I'm afraid of," she returned drily, even as a frisson of electricity danced across her skin at their repartee.

"It may be pleasurable, too," he murmured with a glint in his eye, and then cupped her elbow and steered her forward.

She was disconcerted by how attuned she was to Sawyer and their most casual contact. Had the sexual awareness been caused by their recent kisses, or had it always been there—the unacknowledged reason she'd always kept her distance from him?

A restaurant hostess materialized beside them, and without a word, they were guided to a quiet corner table.

This, Tamara thought, was the kind of service Sawyer was used to by virtue of his wealth, title and high profile. It was the type of service she'd likely be accorded as his wife. She was afraid she could easily become accustomed to the red-carpet treatment.

Tamara slid into her booth seat, Sawyer's lingering touch at her elbow facilitating her way, and Sawyer followed, sitting to her left.

"I'm assuming this meeting is to settle details?" she asked without preamble, settling herself more comfortably on her seat.

"You could say that."

She studied him. "I could—but would it be correct?"

Sawyer's lips twitched. "You mean your father hasn't called you to celebrate his Machiavellian victory?"

She shook her head. "Amazingly, no."

"An admirable and uncharacteristic show of restraint."

She looked at him shrewdly. "Perhaps he was afraid of undermining you."

Sawyer merely laughed, and then reached up to smooth back the hair that had fallen over her shoulder.

She stilled as he touched one of her dangling earrings, set with amethyst stones and Swarovski crystals.

"Is this another of your creations?"

She nodded, and then asked boldly, "Examining your investment?"

He caressed the line of her jaw. "Yes, and it's lovely."

Oh.

Tamara looked away in confusion, and was saved by the approach of a waiter who asked if they would like anything to drink.

After inquiring if wine was her preference, Sawyer smoothly narrowed the choices with the waiter to one, and then turned back to her and settled his hand on her thigh beneath the table. "Does that meet with your approval?"

Feeling the warm weight of Sawyer's hand moving along her thigh, she stuttered assent.

Sawyer looked at her innocently. "Is there something else you'd like, Tamara?"

"What?"

Sawyer's eyes laughed at her. "Is there something else you'd like to drink?"

She looked up at the waiter. "No—thank you."

When they were alone again, Tamara frowned at Sawyer. "What are you doing?"

"You mean this?" Underneath the table, Sawyer's hand clasped hers, and then with his other hand, he slid a ring on her finger.

Tamara felt her heart slow and beat louder.

"A gift from the family vault," Sawyer said. "I hope you like it."

She swallowed and searched Sawyer's gaze, but she read nothing but unadulterated desire there.

She knew, of course, that she and Sawyer were engaged—in a manner of speaking. But the weight of the ring brought the reality of it forcefully back to her.

Slowly, she lifted her hand and rested it on the tablecloth. A beautiful diamond ring in an open-work setting twinkled in the light. Two sapphire baguettes and two accent diamonds adorned either side.

It was a breathtaking piece of jewelry. The diamond was large and undoubtedly flawless, and the open design gave the ring a deceptively modern feel.

"It's a good complement to the earrings you're wearing," Sawyer said with studied solemnity. "It's not a modern piece, but I hope you like it."

She looked up. "Really, it isn't necessary for a pretend marriage—"

"Yes, it is," he said firmly. "The only question is whether you like the ring. I know your tastes tend to the contemporary."

"I love it," she confessed. "It's a creation that any designer would be proud of. The lattice work is timeless and beautiful."

Her response seemed to satisfy him. "I'm glad. The ring was a gift to my great-grandmother, but I had it reset. The original center stone was a sapphire."

Tamara looked down at her hand again. The ring was a tangible sign of her bargain with Sawyer.

"You'll get used to it," he said.

Startled, she glanced up.

He appeared amused for a moment. "I meant the ring. You'll get used to the weight of the ring."

Tamara rued the fact that Sawyer looked as if he'd guessed what was on her mind.

She angled her hand back and forth. "It's exquisite."

"As is its wearer."

She shifted in her seat. She was uncertain how to handle Sawyer. Was he just practicing his romantic technique for the benefit of onlookers?

She wanted to make some acerbic reply about leaving his false devotion for an occasion when they had a real audience, but somehow the words stuck in her throat. Instead, she found herself succumbing to the effect of his nearness and seductive words more than she cared to admit.

"What was the occasion for the gift originally?" she asked, striving to keep the conversation on an even keel.

Sawyer looked suddenly mischievous. "Do you really want to know?"

She raised her brows inquiringly.

"The birth of my great-grandmother's sixth and last child."

Her eyes widened. "Oh, well…"

"Quite." His eyes laughed at her. "One doesn't get to be the twelfth in a direct line of successive earls without ample fertility along the way."

"Perhaps you should be seeking a woman who will better accommodate you in the…fecundity department."

His eyes crinkled. "Perhaps you suit my needs just fine."

She was unsettled by his cryptic reply, but before she could respond, he picked up her ring hand and raised it to his mouth, kissing the pad of each finger individually.

Her eyes widened as a shiver chased through her.

"Someone I know just walked into the restaurant," he murmured, a twinkle in his eyes.

She shot him a skeptical look. "Of course."

"You doubt me?"

She extracted her hand from his loose grip. "Should I?"

Sawyer chuckled, and just then a waiter materialized with a bread basket, followed by their regular server with their wine.

When they were both sipping Pinot Grigio, Tamara attempted to put their conversation on a more businesslike footing. "Tell me about the details that you've obviously called me here to discuss."

He arched a brow. "Your patience has run out? Very well, let's start with Pink Teddy Designs. How much is your lease costing you?"

She relaxed a little, lowering her shoulders. So Sawyer had come here to make good on his promises.

"Too much," she repeated.

"It's a fashionable address—an astute business move."

"Thank you."

"I'll cosign your lease renewal."

Her eyes widened. "How did—?"

He looked at her quizzically. "How did I know the lease was your most pressing concern, you mean? A few discreet inquiries to the landlord netted information on current rents—and the fact that they were going up."

"Lovely," she said acerbically. "I didn't realize my lease was information available to the press!"

Sawyer's lips twisted wryly. "It's not, but I happen to know the head of Rockridge Management."

She made a disgruntled reply.

"You'll also need a cash infusion."

Tamara compressed her lips. Knowing it was best not to look a gift horse in the mouth, however, she forced herself to hold her tongue.

Sawyer considered her. "How does two million dollars for initial financing sound?"

Tamara swallowed. She'd only fantasized about having that kind of cash on hand.

"No strings attached?" she queried.

Sawyer inclined his head in acknowledgment.

Of course, she reminded herself, they both knew that Sawyer wouldn't expect repayment of the money. She had bargained away something else. She'd agreed to a sham marriage.

She cleared her throat. "Thank you...I think. I can promise I'll put the money to good use." And then because she didn't want him to have the impression that she was completely without resources, she added, "I just met with a client this morning, actually."

When Sawyer looked at her inquiringly, she elaborated, "It was a hedge-fund wife who recently opened her own boutique in the Hamptons. She bought a bracelet for herself and selected a few other pieces to carry in her store."

Just then their waiter reappeared, and asked if they were ready to order.

Tamara belatedly realized she hadn't even looked at the menu, but because she'd been to Balthazar before, she ordered the smoked salmon from memory. Sawyer, after a few idle inquiries of their waiter, ordered the grilled branzini.

Afterward, Tamara braced herself and looked at Sawyer squarely. "I suppose we should discuss the wedding itself."

He smiled faintly. "I'll leave the details to you. I understand many women have preconceived ideas of what their wedding should look like."

Yes, and in her case, the idea had never been a sham marriage contracted to a very proper British earl.

On top of it all, Sawyer was also a press baron in her father's mold. She could hardly get any closer to exactly what she *didn't* want.

Sawyer studied her. "It seems only fitting, though, that the marriage of the Earl and Countess of Melton occur at Gantswood Hall, the ancestral home of the earls of Melton."

Tamara resisted pointing out that it was hardly necessary to go to such trouble for what would be a short-lived marriage. But then again, she'd been half expecting Sawyer's proposition of a proper British wedding. "Very well. I suppose the sooner, the better."

Sawyer's lips quirked. "Anxious, are you?"

"The sooner we begin, the sooner the corporate merger will occur and we can be done with this."

"How about next week then?"

Tamara shook her head. "Pia would have a heart attack. I already asked her to help plan the wedding. Three weeks."

"You and Pia Lumley are close."

It wasn't a question, but a statement. Tamara nodded anyway. "Pia is a dear friend and one of the best bridal consultants around. She also needs all the help that she can get now that—" her voice darkened "—your fiendish friend the Marquess of Easterbridge ruined Belinda's wedding day."

Sawyer laughed. "'Fiendish friend'? You certainly have a way with alliteration."

"Don't change the subject," Tamara snapped back. "Your friends seem to come in one stripe only—namely, villainous."

Sawyer arched a brow.

"I suppose you're chummy with the Duke of Hawkshire, too?"

"Yes, but not with his alias, Mr. Fielding."

"Very funny."

"Since we're on the subject of our marriage," Sawyer said drily, "what have you told your friends?"

"Pia and Belinda?" Tamara responded. "They know the truth, and they've already said they'll be at any wedding to support me."

"Splendid."

"We'll need a referee if, as I assume, your titled compatriots will make an appearance, too."

Sawyer inclined his head. "I imagine Hawk and Colin will be there, schedules permitting."

"Everyone else, including my mother and sisters," Tamara said determinedly, "will believe that for reasons known only to me, I've decided that you are Mr. Right."

"Since Hawk has already claimed the moniker Mr. Fielding, I'll settle for Mr. Right without qualm," Sawyer quipped.

Tamara eyed him doubtfully. "Well, I'm glad that's all resolved—anything else?"

"Since you mention it—"

Tamara tensed. "Yes?"

"There is the small matter of where we'll reside after the wedding."

Tamara felt her stomach plummet. Why hadn't she thought of such an obvious and all too important detail?

"I'll keep my business in SoHo," she said automatically.

"Right," Sawyer agreed, "but we won't convince anyone

that we're serious about this marriage unless you move into my town house after the wedding."

Share a roof with Sawyer? They could barely share a *meal* without sparks flying.

"I suppose I can bear it for a short while," she responded in a disgruntled tone. "Will I have my own wing?"

Sawyer laughed at her sudden hopefulness. "Why don't you come see? It occurs to me you've never been to my home, and that's a detail that should be rectified as early as possible. In fact, what are you doing the rest of the afternoon?"

She wanted to lie. She wanted to say she had a slew of meetings. But if Sawyer could make time in his busy CEO schedule, her demurral would hardly ring true. And besides, he had a point about her becoming familiar with the place where she'd soon be living.

"I'm free," she disclosed reluctantly.

Sawyer smiled. "Fantastic. We'll ride up there right after lunch. My car is outside."

The waiter arrived with their food, and as the conversation turned to more mundane topics, Tamara had time at leisure to reflect on what she'd gotten herself into.

Was it too late to back out now?

Seven

Tamara wanted to hate everything about Sawyer's life, but she was finding it impossible to do so. Instead, she clung tenaciously to indifference—was it too much to ask?

It was bad enough that Sawyer himself was demonstrating remarkable skill at seduction. Must his lifestyle be an added lure?

Tamara discovered that Sawyer's town house was a four-story structure on a prime block in the East 80s. The limestone facade was set off by black wrought-iron flower boxes at the windows and a matching black front gate. Shrubbery concealed from prying eyes the garden that ran along one side of the residence.

And in an unusual setup for Manhattan, Sawyer's town house boasted its own garage, enabled by the residence's prime corner location.

Except for a few minor details, the house might have been a transplant from London's fashionable Mayfair district—just like its owner.

A middle-aged, uniformed employee came hurrying out the front door and down the front steps of the town house, and Sawyer handed his car keys to him.

"You might as well garage the car, Lloyd," Sawyer said. "I don't know how long I'll be home."

The man inclined his head. "Very well, my lord."

Sawyer glanced from Lloyd to Tamara and back. "Lloyd, this is Ms. Tamara Kincaid, my fiancée."

Without missing a beat, Lloyd said gravely, "Welcome, Ms. Kincaid. May I offer my utmost felicitations on your engagement?"

Tamara stopped herself from saying that felicitations weren't necessary. Instead, she shook Lloyd's hand and accepted his congratulations before he got into Sawyer's black Porsche Cayenne.

She turned to Sawyer. "What? No Bentley? No valet named Jeeves?"

Sawyer smiled briefly. "The Bentley is at my country estate. I sometimes prefer to drive myself, so Lloyd has time on his hands. There's also a butler, housekeeper and part-time chef, whom you'll soon meet, but no valet."

He added teasingly, "I like to keep things a little democratic when I'm stateside."

Tamara nodded at the house. "I'd have assumed a bachelor like you would prefer a penthouse co-op."

"I find it hard to completely shake the habits of an English country gentleman, even in New York," Sawyer said as his hand cupped her elbow and he guided her toward the front steps. "I hope you like the town house nevertheless."

"It has an understated elegance," she said. "It's...very attractive."

Understated elegance shouldn't appeal to her, but it did. Sawyer was obviously rich as Croesus, and it was hard to withstand the beauty that money sometimes bought.

In Sawyer's case, Tamara grudgingly admitted, generations

of wealth came with good taste that meant he didn't flaunt his money, so beauty didn't shade into gaudiness.

When had she developed an appreciation for low-key charm? Her mind went back to her meeting this morning with the hedge-fund wife. *The bigger, the better* appeared to be that client's motto. Sawyer just seemed appealing in comparison, she told herself.

When she and Sawyer stepped inside the town house's cool foyer, she took in the gilded mirror on one wall, the crystal chandelier overhead and the black-and-white tiled floor.

Sawyer's cell phone rang, and he fished it out of the inside pocket of his suit jacket. "Excuse me a moment. It's work, I'm sure."

Tamara turned away. She was grateful for the interruption actually. She needed the reminder that like her father, Sawyer was tethered to a demanding business—a business for which he was marrying her.

A middle-aged woman stepped from the back of the house, an inquiring look on her face as she took in the tableau before her.

Tamara extended her hand. "Hello, I'm Tamara, Sawyer's fiancée."

She didn't care what the proper etiquette was for a future countess. This one greeted the household help with her first name.

Tamara watched as the chestnut-haired woman briefly looked surprised before her face settled back into a pleasant expression.

Were all the members of Sawyer's household so well trained? Or perhaps, Tamara thought hopefully, they were inured to shock by his various escapades.

"Oooh, gracious!" the woman before her said with a British accent as she shook Tamara's hand. "We thought Lord Melton would never settle down. A crafty one, he is!"

"So true," Tamara responded.

Sawyer sauntered out of the foyer and into a nearby room, still with his cell phone pressed to his ear.

"I'm Beatrice, the housekeeper," the woman said. "The butler—"

"Alfred?" Tamara inquired drolly.

Beatrice hesitated, looking momentarily perplexed. "No, Richard, my husband. He's running an errand at the moment."

Tamara gave a studied sigh. No Jeeves the valet, no superhero's butler named Alfred.

Beatrice clasped her hands together in front of her chest. "I've been praying that Lord Melton would finally find happiness and settle down."

Tamara didn't know about the finding happiness part, but Sawyer had definitely decided to acquire a countess. "Lord Melton is certainly fortunate that those nearest to him have him in their prayers."

The devil.

Beatrice threw her a surprisingly perceptive look. "And why not? He's been a fair, kind and generous employer."

"Have you thought about writing ad copy, Beatrice?" Tamara quipped.

Beatrice laughed lightly. "Oh, you're simply perfect! Exactly the person I've been praying for. You'll do very well here, miss."

"It's Tamara, please."

Tamara wanted to protest that she wasn't perfect at all. And, she wouldn't be around long enough to need to worry about how she'd fare.

She wasn't the answer to Sawyer's prayers in any way but one—namely, the bride who would net him Kincaid News.

Beatrice leaned forward conspiratorially. "We use the name Sawyer when we're not around guests."

Wonderful, Tamara thought. She'd made jabs about Sawyer's loftiness, but he was turning out to have egalitarian tendencies to rival any new money Silicon Valley plutocrat. And his housekeeper *liked* him.

She grasped at any straw she could think of. "Tell me he owns a custom-built submarine and employs someone just to shine his shoes."

Beatrice shook her head, her expression sympathetic. "He's been known to toss his own clothes in the washing machine."

At that moment, Sawyer reentered the foyer, pocketing his cell phone. "Ah, Tamara, I see you've met my indomitable housekeeper."

"Yes."

Beatrice smiled. "And I've met your lovely fiancée. I'm absolutely delighted to offer my congratulations, my lord—"

"Sawyer," Tamara corrected sardonically.

"I'm going to give Tamara a tour of the house, Beatrice."

"Of course." Beatrice turned to Tamara. "I hope you'll feel readily at home here. Please don't hesitate to let me know if there's anything you need."

After Beatrice departed, Tamara discovered on her tour with Sawyer that his house was decorated in an English style, with furniture from the eighteenth and nineteenth centuries blended with more modern pieces. Lively flower patterns on the upholstery contrasted with stripes and solids.

She wanted to hate everything, but unfortunately she was too knowledgeable not to appreciate tastefulness and elegance.

And the house was intimate. Yes, she could identify several valuable objets d'art and a couple of Matisses—Belinda would love them—but the Gainsborough portraits of family ancestors and the Ming dynasty vases had obviously been kept at the historic family home set among thousands of rolling acres in the English countryside. But even with its nod to English décor, this town house was more the home of a twenty-first century entrepreneur than of an aristocrat with a centuries-old title.

After she and Sawyer had passed through the front parlor and dining room, they went downstairs to the kitchen and servants' rooms. There, she was introduced to André, the chef.

Thank goodness, Tamara thought, for the French chef. At least one person lived up to stereotype.

Afterward, she and Sawyer took a private elevator to the upper floors.

"There are six bedrooms on two floors here," Sawyer said.

"I'll take the one farthest from you," Tamara replied. "In fact, since I won't be here for long, and I'd really prefer to remain inconspicuous. What about the maid's room in the attic?"

Sawyer grinned, but Tamara didn't like his too-knowing expression.

"There is no servant's bedroom in the attic. That's only on my Gloucestershire estate," Sawyer deadpanned.

"How unfortunate."

A smile continued to play at Sawyer's lips. "Wouldn't you like to judge all the rooms and decide which one is to your liking?"

Suddenly, Tamara became acutely aware that she and Sawyer were on this floor of the house all by themselves, and Sawyer was surveying her with lazy amusement, a gleam in his eye.

She raised her chin. "Like Goldilocks, you mean? No, thank you!"

Especially since one of those rooms belonged to Sawyer himself. She didn't intend to be his latest sexual conquest—even if she was married to him.

"One bowl of porridge may be too hot, another may be too

cold," Sawyer teased. "One bed may be too big, another may be too small and another may be…just right."

His eyes laughed at her, and he murmured, "Am I remembering the story correctly?"

Damn Sawyer. He'd somehow injected sexual innuendo into a fairy tale.

"I'm not so discriminating," she said, tight-lipped.

Sawyer quirked a brow. "Really? Let's put it to the test."

His hand enveloped hers, and he gently tugged her forward as he pushed open the bedroom door closest to them.

"What are you doing?" she demanded, her voice only slightly breathless.

Peripherally, she noticed they'd stepped into a room with a four-poster queen-size bed and furniture in a gleaming walnut.

Sawyer spun her forward in a dancelike move, and she landed, sitting, on the side of the bed.

Sawyer smiled. "What about this one, Goldilocks?"

"You're ridiculous!"

"Not me, the bed. Too firm, or too soft?"

She bounced off the bed. "Neither!"

"Just right, then?" he said, irrepressibly. "Are you quite sure?"

Before Tamara could react, Sawyer sat on the bed himself, and pulled her back down to him, his mouth settling on hers.

Oh. All through lunch, she'd tried so hard *not* to think about kissing Sawyer.

He kissed, she acknowledged again, in the same way he did everything else in his life—with an intensity and lazy self-assurance that was hard to resist.

Sawyer's hands came up to either side of her face, anchoring her, his fingers threading into her hair.

He caressed her mouth with his in slow, leisurely strokes.

"Your mouth drives me crazy," he muttered, and then

stroked the pad of his thumb over her bottom lip. "It's these lush, pouty lips."

"Thanks very much! You make me sound like a stripper or a porn star."

He smiled. "Don't ever disguise them with lipstick."

She sucked in a breath, but before she could say anything, Sawyer was off the bed and pulling her with him again.

"Where are we going?" she asked on a laughing gasp.

She'd never seen Sawyer let go like this. It was so not in character.

Okay, who was she kidding? It was *thrilling,* and she couldn't help responding to it.

"There are five more bedrooms," Sawyer said as he strode across the hall, leading her by the hand. "This one is mine."

Inside his bedroom, he swung her to face him.

Tamara got a general impression of a four-poster king-size bed, more gleaming dark wood and a distinctly masculine feel.

Then her gaze landed on Sawyer again.

"Oh, no," she said breathlessly, shaking her head at the look in his eyes.

Purposely, he advanced on her, and she backed up until the bedpost stopped her retreat.

Why had she never noticed Sawyer's raw masculinity until recently? Even in a conservative business suit, his tie in place, he looked impossibly sexy. The rakish look in his eyes made her weak-kneed.

A sizzling warmth suffused her. Her breasts tightened, and a heavy ache pooled between her legs.

Maybe before she hadn't wanted to see Sawyer as he was. Maybe *this* was the real reason she'd kept him at a distance.

She itched to caress the firm line of his jaw and the strong column of his neck. She curled her fingers into the palm of her hand to stop herself from doing so.

Sawyer gave her a sexy smile. "What are you thinking?"

"What am I thinking?" she tried, thinking one of them had to hold on to sanity. "Isn't the question, what are you doing?"

He was too close. The inches between them crackled with electricity.

Sawyer's smile widened. "Perhaps I've realized that I'd enjoy having you as my wife in every way."

"Thanks very much!"

"How long has it been for you?" he murmured. "I know you and what's-his-name weren't intimate."

Her mouth dropped open, and then snapped shut. "Tom, his name is Tom. And I'm not discussing this with you."

Sawyer's smile turned lazy and knowing. "That long, then?"

He touched her, smoothing the backs of his fingers down the side of her breast in a gentle caress, and Tamara sucked in a breath.

"Damn you," she whispered.

He slid his hand up her arm, bringing her into his embrace. "Your eyes tell a different story, Goldilocks."

"Oh?" she said, cursing the catch in her voice. "Do tell!"

Sawyer searched her face, arousal stamped on his. "Your eyes are already cloudy with desire."

She tried to look bored, even as the press of his arousal sent a fresh wave of awareness shooting through her. "You're making me sleepy."

Sawyer chuckled before his expression turned seductive and intent again.

"What's the matter, Goldilocks?" he muttered, his head bending toward hers. "Are you finding that this bed is just right?"

And then his mouth met hers again.

He tasted of wine from their meal, and the scent of some expensive and finely-milled English sandalwood soap clung to his skin. The combination was strangely intoxicating. And she yielded to it, her hands running up his arms until she clung to him, her arms around his neck.

Damningly, she didn't think about whether this was *right*. It just felt *good*.

She'd passed the point of reflection and gone on to someplace more elemental.

Sawyer pressed her against the bedpost, his muscled thigh wedging between her legs.

He toyed with her lips, and she moaned with each nip and suck and gentle graze.

"That's right," he approved gutturally. "Let me know how you feel."

His mouth wandered away from hers, tracing along her jaw, and her head fell to one side, exposing her neck for their mutual pleasure.

While he kissed the column of her neck, his hands roamed and molded, running down her sides, from the curve of her breasts to the jut of her hips. In response, her fingers curled into his shoulders with pleasure.

When Sawyer's mouth came back to hers, he slid his hand up under the hem of her dress. Her head fell back, and she moaned again as his hand brushed aside her panties.

They both held still as his hand caressed her, his fingers delving into her moist heat, stroking her. From beneath her lashes, Tamara noticed Sawyer's eyes glitter   n at her, his face intent with arousal.

"Ah, Tamara," he breathed. "Ah, Goldiloc

Sawyer's free hand went to his belt, but then he suddenly stopped, his head tilting.

A moment later, Tamara heard it, too—the unmistakable sound of footsteps.

Someone was coming up the stairs.

Just as Tamara frantically jerked away, Sawyer stepped back, his expression turning smooth and businesslike even as he took care to straighten her dress.

Sawyer was a practiced master of seduction. The thought flashed through her mind a second before she peripherally noticed someone walk past their open doorway.

"I hope you've enjoyed our tour, Tamara," Sawyer said in a voice loud enough to carry.

His eyes laughed down at her, his expression gently mocking.

"Who was that?" Tamara whispered urgently.

Sawyer bent his head toward hers.

"I believe a person sent by the weekly housecleaning service," he said with a grin, matching her low and urgent tone.

Argh. Gathering her dignity, or what remained of it, she stepped away from him so that she was no longer cornered by the bedpost.

"No need to be concerned," Sawyer said. "I'm sure she wouldn't have been too surprised to discover an engaged couple locked in an embrace. Embarrassed, maybe, surprised, no."

Sawyer had acted deftly to avoid embarrassment to an outside employee. Unfortunately, Tamara thought, her own mortification was unabated.

She should be thankful that Sawyer had again been thwarted by the unexpected arrival of a third party. Instead, she was concerned, very concerned, by her reaction and increasing susceptibility to his charms.

"We're not really an engaged couple," she responded with false composure. "Or need I remind you of our agreement?"

Sawyer's eyes narrowed a fraction, but then his lips quirked.

He reached out and smoothed her hair. "What's the harm in a little pleasure along the way?"

What indeed. She took another step back, and he dropped his hand back to his side.

"We don't suit," Tamara said firmly, "and we never will."

His expression turned mocking. "We suited just fine a minute ago—"

She made a sweeping movement with her arm, gesturing to the room around them.

"This is not my world," she said, putting aside her earlier charmed reaction to his town house. "And I'm not going to trade away who I am in exchange for it."

He arched a brow.

"We may need to put on a convincing show that our marriage won't be a complete sham," she continued stubbornly, "but we don't need to be too convincing. And you don't need practice!"

Sawyer gazed at her thoughtfully for a second, and then laughed throatily.

She turned on her heel.

Unfortunately, *this* Goldilocks had made her bed, but she wasn't sure whether she wanted to lie in it.

Eight

Tamara stood at the base of the steps of Gantswood Hall and surveyed the picturesque hills in the distance. From her vantage point, she could see the white dots of grazing sheep on the hillsides under the July sun. The stately home that was Sawyer's ancestral family seat sat amid the Cotswolds, and like most of the neighboring architecture, was made of an inviting honey-colored limestone, worlds away from the bleak, drafty castle she used to imagine him in.

A car that Sawyer had sent to pick her up from the airport stood parked near the front entrance of the Tudor mansion, its driver unloading her luggage.

Tamara breathed in the crisp country air, fragrant with the smell of grass and leaves and fresh streams.

The truth was she hadn't ventured to a stately British country estate since reaching adulthood. Not even to her father's family seat, Dunnyhead. She had been expecting to be put off by the whole experience. She was surprised to find herself...enchanted.

Gantswood Hall lay farther south than Dunnyhead, and its landscape was less bracing, more pastoral. It was the Gloucestershire countryside at its best.

But it was more than the landscape that drew her. A part of her, she acknowledged now, would always remain attached to the British countryside, no matter how many miles and how much time she stayed away. And soon she'd have a new—if temporary—tie to bind her there.

She'd arrived today as Tamara Kincaid, but she would leave as Tamara, Countess of Melton, and she would be addressed as Lady Melton or simply, my lady.

In deference to the mantle she'd opted to assume, she'd dressed conservatively in fawn-colored pants and a sky-blue shirt. She could have, she thought, walked out of an ad for Ralph Lauren.

Absently, she ran her finger over the spot on her shirt that covered the small rose tattoo she'd acquired in an East Village salon a few years ago.

She might have donned the uniform of a British aristocrat, but, she reminded herself, inside she was still the free-spirited designer with a SoHo loft.

Of course, she'd retained possession of said loft only thanks to Sawyer's timely intervention. He'd cosigned her lease renewal and assumed payment of the monthly rent. He'd also deposited a generous sum in Pink Teddy's commercial bank account.

"The first installment," he'd said, acting as if the amount were of little consequence.

The recollection should have made her happy. Instead, she wanted to cringe.

She felt bought.

She shook her head. Why shy away from the truth?

She *had* been bought. She'd had a price and Sawyer had met it.

She surveyed the hills before her, where all matter of

wildlife still roamed. All of it was the domain of the earls of Melton, no doubt at least partially acquired through various dynastic marriages over the centuries.

And now she was about to become the latest Langsford bride. In two days, she'd wear an embroidered lace wedding dress and Kincaid jewels to wed Sawyer in the village chapel. Pia would help make sure everything went off without a hitch.

Though the wedding was to be small, all the immediate family would be in attendance, including her mother and stepfather, Mr. and Mrs. Ward George, her sisters and, of course, her father. On Sawyer's side, his mother, Mrs. Peter Beauregard, and her teenage daughter from her second marriage, Jessica, would be present. And then, of course, there would be Belinda and Pia, and the Marquess of Easterbridge and the Duke of Hawkshire. Adding some buffer to the mix, a number of extended family, a few other friends, some neighbors and Sawyer's closest business associates would also be in attendance.

Tamara tamped down the well of turbulent anticipation. Since she'd never eloped in a Las Vegas wedding chapel, at least they wouldn't have to worry about any former husbands making an appearance.

No, the only concern this time would be the possibility of a runaway bride, Tamara thought with a barely suppressed hysterical laugh.

She replayed her mother's reaction on the phone when she'd announced she was getting married.

Honey, no.

You'll find life as Sawyer's wife absolutely stifling. What has possessed you to even think…?

I hope your father hasn't pressured you.

And then, once it had become apparent Tamara was determined to go through with the marriage, remaining steadily mum about her reasons for doing so other than that she'd fallen for Sawyer Langsford, Susan George had sighed heavily.

I never imagined you'd aspire to status, Tamara. But, darling, I can't fault you if you do. Certainly having married wealth and position has benefited me.

It was Sawyer's wealth she was counting on, Tamara thought now. It was his financial support that had made her agree to this farce of a marriage at all. So why did standing on the steps of his ancestral estate, expecting him to come and greet her at any moment, feel so strangely like coming home?

Tamara heard footsteps behind her, and turned.

Sawyer.

Her heart skipped a beat.

He trotted down the front steps of the house, looking virile in riding boots, form-fitting trousers and an open-collared shirt. A thin sheen of sweat glazed his throat and brow, giving him an air of healthy vibrancy.

Her pulse thrummed in her veins, and she swallowed. *Don't be silly,* she told herself. Sawyer was a cool-headed businessman. And they had made a heartless bargain. *Best remember that.*

There would *not* be a repeat of their romantic interlude at his town house—at least if she could help it.

When Sawyer reached her, he gave her a quick kiss on the lips before she could react.

"Do you ride?" he asked.

"Horses?"

Sawyer's mouth quirked up. "No, taxis." He gestured in the direction of the house. "The stables are beyond the gardens."

"I haven't ridden in ages."

He surveyed her, his topaz eyes missing nothing. "Then tomorrow morning we should see about ending the drought. I'll have riding attire bought for you."

"No need," she responded. "I brought along riding boots and appropriate clothing."

It was a grudging admission. She'd hoped to hold him off with her comment that she didn't ride any longer. But just in case, before she'd left New York, she'd made sure she bought some riding boots and clothes. She'd felt duty-bound to do so by her bargain to play the role of the happy fiancée.

When Sawyer arched a brow, she added somewhat defensively, "I've come prepared to play my part, if nothing else."

Their eyes held for a moment, unspoken meaning stretching the silence between them while her driver walked past with her bags.

"Your belongings will be put in our private set of rooms," Sawyer said.

When Tamara opened her mouth to argue, he added, "We have to maintain the pretense that this marriage is real."

"Yes, after the wedding!"

Sawyer looked amused. "Don't tell me you want to act the role of the blushing bride."

With unfortunate timing, she felt herself flush.

Damn him.

And it didn't help that right now he looked as virile a male specimen as could possibly stride over Gloucestershire's green grass.

"Why not play the role to the hilt?" she flung back.

Especially since in this case it gave her an excuse to maintain some distance from Sawyer.

"You don't need to worry," he said sardonically, though a teasing glint remained in his eyes. "The private rooms are two adjoining suites. The countesses of Melton have all traditionally had their own suites—including a separate bed."

She raised her chin. "How clever of them."

The corners of Sawyer's eyes crinkled. He stepped closer

and habitually tucked back a strand of her hair that had caught the breeze.

"I'm glad you've arrived," he murmured.

She searched his expression, but all she saw was appreciation—and the promise of something more.

Sawyer bent and brushed his lips across hers again.

He tasted of leather and sweat and clean country air, and she involuntarily felt herself sway into him.

When he straightened, his expression was enigmatic. "We might as well start practicing now if we're going to convince our guests this marriage isn't just a brief arrangement."

"Of course," she managed.

His eyes glinted. "Follow me," he said, turning. "I'll show you the house."

They walked up the front steps together and into the cool, dark front hall, where Sawyer hailed an older woman who appeared to be Beatrice's counterpart in England—the housekeeper.

"Ah, Eleanor," Sawyer said. "May I present Ms. Tamara Kincaid, my fiancée?"

As she shook hands with Eleanor, Tamara was careful to disguise her inner turmoil.

Sawyer's greeting had left her unsure of her footing.

Not good. Not good at all.

Early the next morning, Tamara knocked on the partially open door of Sawyer's study before walking inside.

Sawyer looked up at her knock.

He stood, hands braced on hips, behind a massive wood desk at the other end of the room. Sunlight shafted in from the windows, bathing him in a beam of radiance. He looked like a historical lord plotting his next conquest. She quelled the feeling that in this case that might be *her*.

Breathing in deeply, she sauntered farther into the room.

They had missed his study on their tour of the house the day before, though they'd skipped very little else.

As she'd suspected, Gantswood Hall was heavy with the weight of history. The walls of the reception rooms were mounted with Gainsboroughs, van Dycks and other priceless works of art, including portraits of Sawyer's ancestors. Busts and other valuable sculptures dating back hundreds of years were showcased in the halls and entry. Beautiful molded-plaster ceilings added to the ambience of centuries of genteel wealth.

"Do you always stand behind your desk?" she asked now, half expecting to see Sawyer contemplating a battle map—no doubt like ancestors of yore.

"Not always, but sometimes," Sawyer responded, lips curving. "It helps with the restless energy when I'm deliberating something."

"And what would that be?" she asked.

"Some architectural improvements to a set of outlying buildings on the estate," he responded.

While he pushed together papers on his desk, she scanned the room.

Sawyer's study was more or less what she expected it would be. It had beautiful built-in bookshelves and old and valuable artwork. All that was missing, she thought wryly, was a pipe and smoking jacket and the late Alistair Cooke announcing the beginning of *Masterpiece Theatre*.

Interestingly, however, the room displayed what looked like a variety of travel memorabilia, including various framed photos.

She stopped before a bookshelf and examined a wood mask that appeared to be painted with gold and bronze.

"Nepal," Sawyer said.

She glanced at him. "I didn't realize you'd ever been."

"Five years ago. But I did not attempt to scale to the top of Mount Everest, in case you're wondering."

"Of course," she quipped. "You're too busy climbing to various corporate pinnacles."

At his chuckle, she glided on along the line of bookshelves until her eyes landed on a mahogany frame. Bending toward it, she realized it was a photo of a helmeted Sawyer emerging from a tank.

"Embedded with an army unit at the front lines," he elaborated, sauntering toward her.

She arched a brow as she turned to look at him. "Working as a war correspondent is part of your job as head of a news corporation?"

"Only occasionally. Don't tell."

"Far be it for me to ruin your reputation as a stuffy aristocrat."

"After my studies at Cambridge," he said, "I did a brief military service."

"Couldn't escape the family tradition?" She knew many upper-class families still looked upon a military career as a gentleman's calling.

"Didn't want to," he responded, refusing to be drawn in.

She turned away, and seeking a more neutral topic, pointed to a framed photo of him and three people dressed in traditional African garb standing in front of a nondescript building.

"As I recall," Sawyer said, answering her unspoken question, "we had just arrived at the medical station with vaccines after dodging a handful of armed rebels in a Jeep."

"Oh."

She hid her surprise and confusion. Sawyer wasn't supposed to be Indiana Jones disguised as a staid British earl. He might live the news business, but it was clear it went beyond empire-building and down to the trenches. He helped people, and he found and told their stories.

To her chagrin, Sawyer made her occasional volunteer work

serving food in a New York City homeless shelter seem rather insignificant.

"Are you ready to ride?" Sawyer asked.

Why, oh, why, did she have to see sexual suggestion in his words?

He was so close she only had to reach out a hand to feel the hard planes of his chest, or the outline of a muscular thigh beneath form-fitting riding pants.

Sawyer's topaz gaze traveled over her, from her hair caught in a ponytail to her white shirt, snug-fitting pants and polished black boots.

She wet her lips.

Sawyer's eyes came back to hers, too knowing. "You didn't answer my question."

Had they been talking about something?

"Are you ready to ride?" he repeated, his eyes holding a telltale glint.

"Of course."

He took a half step closer. "Good...then there's just one more thing."

"What's that?" she asked with a touch of breathlessness.

He bent his head, and she watched his mouth curve...right before he settled his lips on hers.

Her hand came up to his chest, but before she could use it to keep some physical separation, he captured it in his, drew it aside and laced his fingers with hers.

His mouth moved over hers, and when she would have made to pull away, he pressed her back against the bookcases, settling his body against hers.

He coaxed her into a soul-searching kiss even as his free hand roamed her curves.

Her hand curled around his, and he held her firmly.

He fit against her curves, his hard planes pressing her, molding her, and she could feel his growing arousal. She picked up the faint scent of sandalwood soap underneath that of freshly polished leather.

She didn't want to desire *this*. Desire *him*. But pure need fueled her response.

She responded to his kiss with a growing urgency, her hand plowing through the hair at the back of his head.

As if seizing upon her response, he moved his mouth from hers to trail kisses along her jaw. With an impatient hand, he undid the upper buttons of her shirt, exposing the lace of her bra, and then pressed small, warm kisses against the soft flesh of her throat.

When he moved up to claim her mouth again, his hand molded and squeezed her breast, and she met him greedily.

Sawyer made her feel. She was almost afraid of how much and *what* he made her feel.

It wasn't supposed to be like this. This wasn't part of their agreement.

She made a monumental effort to summon the will to resist.

At that very moment, however, as if Sawyer could read her mind, he drew back.

Sawyer's eyes glittered down at her, and she swallowed, clutching her open blouse with one hand.

He rubbed her lower lip with his thumb. "You look as if you've been thoroughly kissed."

"Thanks to you," she replied.

She had meant it as an accusation, but Sawyer just gave her a slow, satisfied smile.

"Thanks to me," he agreed, his voice still rough with arousal. "No one will doubt we're anything but lovers on the eve of being newlyweds."

The reminder of the status of their *relationship*—if it indeed could be called that—was the last jolt she needed to free herself from their sexual interlude.

"I'll meet you outside," she said tightly.

As she stalked from the room, she could feel Sawyer's gaze on her.

Damn him. How could she call him on his game of seduction when he kept claiming it was no more than that—a game?

Nine

Sawyer stood at the altar waiting for the bride.

He'd started on this road as a means to acquiring Kincaid News. But somewhere along the way, acquiring—no, possessing—Tamara had begun to consume his thoughts.

He wanted her. In his bed. Under him. Moaning, just as she had in his study yesterday before they'd gone horseback riding.

He'd discovered she rode a horse well. *Like a bike,* she'd said. *You never forget.* These days, he was finding her fairly unforgettable, too.

Damn.

His cutaway morning coat wasn't structured to conceal an arousal. If he wasn't careful, he'd be giving the guests in the pews an eyeful.

So far, he had been able to use the excuse of acting like an engaged, albeit not necessarily in love, couple as cover for his real and increasing need to seduce her—a need, he admitted, that he had increasing trouble remembering was tied to his bargain with Kincaid.

The church organ struck up, and a hushed silence fell over the guests. All eyes went to the doors at the back, which swung open to reveal Tamara on the arm of her father.

Sawyer drew in a breath at the sight of her as she started toward him.

She looked magnificent. Her vivid hair was piled up in an elaborate knot, and a delicate diamond tiara, one of the Kincaid family heirlooms, nestled there, matching the diamonds at her ears. Her dress was a strapless ivory lace confection with a full skirt. Gauzy material wrapped around her shoulders like a shrug and tucked into her bodice.

But it was her face that enthralled him. Classical beauty defined her features, her green eyes captivating beneath arched brows, her lips pink and glossy, inviting his kiss.

Sawyer sent a silent apology to the minister standing next to him, because all he wanted at that moment was to pick Tamara up, stride back down the aisle and ravish her.

Instead, he waited patiently until Tamara reached him and Viscount Kincaid kissed her cheek.

Once she put aside her bouquet of tightly-packed roses, he took her hand, claiming her.

He felt a tremor go through her and glanced her way, but her alabaster profile remained composed.

He barely registered the voice of the minister. "We are gathered together…"

He kept Tamara's hand in his, feeling the vital flow of life between them.

The minister led them in their vows, the same ones used in royal weddings. Sawyer felt his eyes crinkle when Tamara delicately repeated "to love and to cherish" and omitted "obey."

For his part, he intended to love and cherish her—in the

full physical sense and as soon as possible. In that way, his vows couldn't be more real.

When it was time for the exchange of rings, he produced a filigreed wedding band of platinum and diamonds and slipped it on her finger. There it joined the diamond engagement ring that he'd given her.

He was glad to see Tamara's lips curve into a faint smile as she looked at the new ring on her finger. He'd debated long and hard before selecting the wedding ring at longstanding Langsford family jewelers Boodle & Dunthorne. He'd wanted a ring that fit Tamara's fashion-forward sense and was impressive enough for the new Countess of Melton. From the look on Tamara's face, he'd made the right choice.

Moments later, Tamara slipped a wedding ring on his finger—the plain platinum band with small grooved edges that he'd ordered.

When it was time to kiss the bride, he settled his lips on hers with satisfaction, letting her glimpse his simmering passion and feel the promise of more.

He was joined to Tamara now, and somehow it didn't feel just like a means to an end. Except, of course, if that end was the wedding night.

Tamara sipped her champagne, adjusting to the weight of two magnificent rings on her finger—and adjusting to the enormity of what she'd just done.

Married to Sawyer. She was now the Countess of Melton.

She was seated among the seventy-odd invited guests in the main dining room of Gantswood Hall, where the traditional wedding breakfast was taking place.

Thankfully, she thought, glancing around, this whole affair would soon be over. Pia was ignoring the Duke of Hawkshire, and Belinda and Colin sat like two combatants at an impasse.

The remaining wedding guests and a roving photographer were convenient buffers.

In fact, the only person who appeared in the best of spirits was her father.

As if on a cue from her thoughts, Viscount Kincaid pushed back his chair and stood.

"A toast," her father announced, raising his glass.

Tamara nearly groaned aloud, and everyone else dutifully reached for their glasses.

This, Tamara thought, was destined to be her life if she stayed married to Sawyer. There were all sorts of issues of protocol, precedence and etiquette that she would need to be aware of. She would need to conform to certain rules after years of priding herself on being a nonconformist.

True, she'd enjoyed her horseback ride yesterday. True, she found Sawyer's kisses more potent than any other man's. But they were all wrong for each other.

She pulled her mind back, realizing her father was looking at her, for once in her life, with approval.

"To Tamara, my dear daughter, and Sawyer, whom I proudly welcome as my son-in-law," her father said. "May your marriage be long and fruitful."

Tamara refused to glance at Sawyer. *If only her father knew.* This time he'd met his match in ruthlessness.

"And may you find a lasting happiness together."

Tamara hid her surprise. She wasn't expecting *that* toast. Looking at her father's face, though, she realized he meant it.

"To Tamara and Sawyer," the other guests said in unison, saluting them before sipping their champagne.

Tamara set down her glass, and then before she could react, Sawyer picked up her hand and raised it to his lips.

"I shall endeavor to use my very best efforts to make Tamara happy," he announced, gazing into her eyes.

She could almost read the end of his sentence in his tawny gaze. *In bed.*

Extricating her hand, she gave a fixed smile. "Sawyer, you've already made me happy."

She thought of her loft back in New York and her dreams for Pink Teddy, and banished all thoughts of Sawyer's seductiveness.

Sawyer's amused expression was all too knowing, and she angled her chin up stubbornly.

She refused to be vanquished over plates of salmon in a delicate cream sauce with a side of asparagus spears.

A door connected the master's and mistress's private quarters at Gantswood Hall.

Sawyer contemplated the door now. He'd just showered, his hair still damp as he pulled on a pair of cotton pajama bottoms.

In centuries past, the door, which connected the earl's and countess's sitting rooms, had been the gateway through which the lord and lady of the house were expected to meet to do their sacred duty—namely, to beget heirs.

It was how his father had been conceived, and his father's father and so on down the line.

He himself, on the other hand, had by all reports been conceived in one of the luxury hotel suites at Claridge's, soon after his parents had embarked on their impetuous and tempestuous union.

His aristocratic father had married a free-spirited American socialite and heiress, and the marriage had been a—thankfully brief—disaster.

The thought gave him a brief moment's pause. He was well-versed in the pitfalls of marrying a woman unsuited to the role of countess.

But he'd struck his bargain with Viscount Kincaid. And even in this day and age, he had a duty to secure the earldom by producing a successor to the responsibilities of his hereditary peerage.

And the truth was he was as impatient to consummate his marriage as any bridegroom. He'd been suffering the pangs of frustrated desire for his bride for too long.

Tonight, God help him, there'd be no untimely interruptions by sad-sack boyfriends or unsuspecting household help.

Tonight, he'd seduce Tamara.

With that thought, he strode to the door and tapped lightly. After a moment, trying again and receiving no answer, he turned the knob and entered.

Tamara's sitting room was empty, and so, for that matter, was what he could see of her bedroom through the doorway.

Where was she?

It was nearing midnight, and they'd both had a long day. After the wedding breakfast, they'd continued to socialize with various guests, until they'd seen a number of their visitors depart.

Sawyer walked farther into Tamara's bedroom.

Her personal belongings lay about, and his eyes came to rest on the wedding dress that was draped on a rose-and-gold-striped armchair.

Walking over, he picked up the dress and brought it up to his face, closing his eyes and inhaling deeply.

A hint of jasmine.

A little exotic, a lot erotic.

His body tightened.

Allowing the lacy gown to drop back onto the chair, he let his eyes follow a path of strewn clothing from where he was standing to the bathroom door.

A pair of red panties, a white garter...

His blood began to hum.

He could hear the shower running now, and his feet took him to the bathroom door.

He didn't even think. He opened the door and walked in—

side, and immediately focused on Tamara's silhouette visible through the fogging shower door, her dark-red hair partly wet.

Her face was turned up to the shower jet, her eyes closed as soapy water ran in rivulets over her shoulders and disappeared beneath the steam that partially concealed her from his avid gaze.

Sawyer felt his blood pound harder in his veins. His body was revved, ready on a hair trigger to seek mind-blowing pleasure with her.

At that moment, Tamara turned her head and saw him.

He watched her eyes go wide with shocked surprise.

They stared at each other while the steam continued to rise between them.

Then she slapped her hand on the handle of the shower and shut off the water.

"What are you doing here?" she demanded as she turned to face him again.

"I live here, if you'll recall."

He wanted to enjoy the show. *Step out of the stall slowly.*

He reached for one of the plush beige towels hanging nearby and moved toward the shower door.

Her green eyes flashed, as bright as any fine emeralds. But despite the performance, he could read her nervousness.

"You haven't answered my question," she said.

"We need to discuss what we're doing tomorrow," he replied. "This is the only time we'll have to speak privately. We still have guests—including your father—who'll expect us to act like content, if not lovestruck, newlyweds."

It wasn't a complete lie. They did need to talk.

But his body damned conversation. It wanted something more elemental from her.

"Out," she demanded.

"Precisely what I was thinking." He held the towel before him. "I won't look."

She hesitated, and then chin held high, opened the stall door and stepped out.

He lowered the towel, and she sucked in a breath.

He drank in the sight. Her shoulders and arms were sculpted, her waist tiny. And her breasts...

He swallowed. *Beautiful.* Her nipples were erect and rosy, beckoning to him in their tightness.

And that damned rose tattoo...

"You said you wouldn't look!"

His lips twitched. "The sight proved irresistible."

Her eyes rounded, the sexual current oscillating between them.

"Tamara, all grown-up," he said roughly. "You do make an exquisite countess."

Her lips parted, her eyes moving from his bare chest and down to his arousal.

The part of his brain still functioning was a bit amused by her loss for words. The other part took satisfaction in the evidence that she was just as affected as he was.

He let the towel fall from his grasp to the floor.

The curls at the apex of her thighs were just as dark and lushly red as her hair.

Heaven.

He reached out and drew the pad of his forefinger over her nipple.

She gasped, and he hoped the sensation was as exquisite as she gave every evidence of it being.

Her eyes flashed. "Looking for some novelty, Sawyer? A shag with someone who's not your usual type?"

"With someone who's my wife."

"In name only!"

"Labels are only as meaningful as we allow them to be."

She bent to snatch up the towel, but he was just as fast... bending with her and dragging her into the shelter of his arms as his mouth fastened on hers.

Lips locked together, they rose slowly.

He folded her close, and her arms inched around his neck. The wetness that still clung to her skin dampened them both, joining them, as his arousal settled against her.

Ever since their first kiss, the attraction between them had been combustible, and now it seemed they were both powerless as it flamed to life again.

His hand slipped down her back, rubbed over her derriere and back up again. *She felt so good.*

He moved his mouth from hers, trailing kisses across her cheek and down to her throat.

"You're a moth to the flame, aren't you, Sawyer?" she taunted softly.

He lifted his head, and looked into her green eyes, bright with desire and provocation.

"Does it get boring for you buttoned-down types?" Tamara asked.

"Never when you're around."

A hint of vulnerability flashed across her face, but it was quickly gone. "Is that a compliment?"

"A promise."

She opened her mouth, but he swallowed her response with his, breathing in the scent of jasmine that lingered lightly on her skin.

He slid his hand over her thigh, lifting it and wrapping it around him.

He let his hands dance over her body, plying her with pleasure until he felt her relax. Only then did he bend over her, cupping and nuzzling her breasts.

He laved one nipple and then the other, heard her moan, and then fastened his mouth over one breast.

Her hands tangled in his hair, and her moan fueled his ardor.

He lifted his mouth to move to the other breast. "You're so responsive."

"We unconventional types usually are."

Her reply made him smile.

"Show me," he urged, planting a quick nip on the rose tattoo that always drew him.

She was obviously set on reminding him how different she was from his usual type, because she thought he was after a quick coupling with novelty value.

Instead he... Well, he would love to demonstrate to her just how *novel* an experience theirs could be. There was so much passion between them that he couldn't wait to explore.

But then he thought unexpectedly of that hint of vulnerability he'd seen earlier.

Damnation.

He wanted her. But if he took her, she'd think it was because she was the flavor of the day.

The movement of her hand cut into his thoughts. He felt the flutter of a caress along his arousal, and then another, and bit back a groan.

Her hand slid up and down along the length of him through his pajama bottoms, again and again.

Hot and heady sensation coursed through him. His breath became more labored and he felt his muscles bunch, readying his body for release. He needed to be inside her. Except he couldn't.

Hell and damn.

He turned his head and growled next to her ear, "You, too."

Then he cupped her intimately, his hand delving into the damp curls at the juncture of her thighs, interrupting her hand in its steady motion on him.

After a moment, he slipped a finger inside her and felt her body clasp around him, pulling tight as a bow.

They both groaned with satisfaction.

He moved his thumb, finding the nub hidden in her curls with unerring accuracy, and pressed.

She gasped, and then her hand reached up to grasp his arm. "Sawyer…"

"Yes, say my name," he replied thickly.

He pressed forward, feeling her tremble with anticipation.

And in the next instant, she shattered, shaking and crying out, her body racked with waves of pleasure that seeped from her skin to his.

He held her, and moments later, feeling her heart still pounding, he moved damp hair back from her face and brushed his lips across hers.

A promise.

"Sawyer," she said scratchily.

But he wasn't done.

He knelt and cupped her bottom, bringing her against his mouth. He gave her an intimate kiss, one that had her body rising up to meet him while the breath seemed to leave her lungs in a whoosh.

Soon, she came apart again, this time against his mouth, and his palms smoothed down her legs, easing the tremor that signaled her release.

When he finally rose, his eyes locked on hers. Her face was flushed, her lips full and red, and her eyes wide and glazed.

He stifled an oath. His body still hurt with his unspent release. But in her eyes, there was still that vulnerability, reminding him how easily she could be hurt by what he did.

He bent and handed her the fallen towel, though many of the droplets that had clung to her skin had evaporated—no doubt due to their steamy encounter.

Then silently, he turned and walked from the room before he gave in to temptation.

Ten

With experienced precision, Tamara used the tweezers to set the opal in place, and then sat back and sighed.

She removed her visor, whose attached magnifying glass she had previously turned up, and rubbed the back of her neck.

She stared out at the majestic English countryside beckoning to her from between the damask drapes of her sitting room. It was early, before eight, but soon she'd have no choice but to face Sawyer again.

After having slept badly, she'd resorted to one of her better relaxation techniques. There was something soothing, almost tranquilizing, about jewelry-making. Like knitting, it kept the hands busy while allowing the mind to wander.

She always traveled with a jewelry project or two, just so she'd have something to turn to if necessary—and with Sawyer around, it was proving *very* necessary.

Methodically, she put away her implements, placing pliers and tweezers back in their carrying cases. She closed the box holding semiprecious gemstones, and put away her portable metal-working kit.

She hadn't heard any movement in the earl's suite next door, so Sawyer was either sleeping soundly or had woken up before she'd gotten out of bed.

For her part, she had tossed and turned last night, willing herself to sleep.

Despite having had not one, but two, orgasms in Sawyer's arms, she'd gone to bed alone and feeling frustrated and out of sorts.

How dare Sawyer surprise her while she was in the shower? How dare he bring her sexual fulfillment—not once but twice? How dare he leave without explanation?

She was so confounded by his behavior she didn't know what she was most upset about.

How dare Sawyer twist her in knots.

Of course, she'd been an active participant in their romantic interlude. She'd told herself she was going to remind him just how incompatible they were—the bohemian, wayward daughter and the aristocratic lord. But events hadn't unfolded in the way she'd expected.

Her cheeks flamed as she replayed the scene from last night. Sawyer had shown a greater mastery of her body and all its pleasure points than any man she'd ever known.

And then he'd left abruptly.

Was it because he'd come to his senses and realized the two of them were, in fact, a crazy pairing?

She felt an unexpected squeeze around her heart.

Her cell phone beeped, indicating she'd just received a text message, and she got up to retrieve it from where it was recharging on a nearby table.

When she reached her phone, she realized the message was from Sawyer.

Tour the Cotswolds with me at eleven. The guests will expect it.

Before she could reply to the text, however, she heard a discreet knock on her sitting room door and went to answer it.

When she opened her door, she discovered Sage, one of the maids she'd been introduced to, standing in the hall.

"My lady," Sage said, "his lordship sent me to attend to you."

"Thank you," she replied, wondering what Sage thought of the lord and lady of the house communicating at arm's length on the morning after their wedding. "However, I do not require anything at the moment."

She looked down at herself. She was wearing an oversized T-shirt and well-worn pajama bottoms. She hadn't even bothered with a robe. No doubt about it. She was hardly countess material.

For Sage's benefit, though, she added, "But please tell his lordship I will meet him for our tour as planned."

Sage hesitated for a moment, as if perplexed, but then nodded and retreated.

As Tamara closed the door, she thought about how Sawyer was a blend of the modern and archaic. He'd sent a text message *and* a lady's maid within moments of each other. He had a Manhattan town house suited to a media baron *and* an English country estate worthy of an earl.

But, she reminded herself, they were still hardly compatible. Sure, he'd surprised her on several fronts, but just because Sawyer had shown signs of being less buttoned-down than she'd dismissed him as being, it didn't mean they weren't oil and water.

She was thoroughly modern. More than slightly bohemian. Independent and American.

She and Sawyer were proving compatible in the bedroom, but as she well knew, much more was involved in a successful marriage.

* * *

As Tamara walked alongside Sawyer through the nearest village, she couldn't help but be impressed again with the natural beauty of this part of Britain.

Traditional thatched-roof cottages clung together in little groups under the late-morning sun, and everywhere the local golden limestone was in evidence, from low-lying walls to the exterior of homes and businesses.

The setting was picturesque, and it fired her imagination. She wanted to go home—no, sit in the fields—with her sketchbook and design something inspired by the local landscape.

The locals all hailed Sawyer by name, and he introduced her as his new countess.

This meet-and-greet, she thought, had been Sawyer's purpose in proposing a walking tour of the local village.

Fortunately, she'd dressed for the role of the new mistress of Gantswood Hall. Before she'd left New York, she'd made sure to buy clothes that would be more appropriate to wear during her trip than her usual attire. Her flowered blouse, A-line blue skirt and ballerina flats complemented Sawyer's blue shirt and beige pants.

Yet she'd refused to disguise herself completely. Her favorite self-designed earrings completed her outfit.

She'd expected Sawyer to frown at the sight of such loud accent pieces. Instead, strangely enough, he'd smiled.

She and Sawyer left the baker's shop and sauntered down the street, and Sawyer picked up her hand, lacing his fingers with hers.

At the moment, there was no one approaching them, so she had a brief window during which to speak her mind.

"I'm hardly going to be the Countess of Melton long enough for all these introductions," she protested in a low voice.

Sawyer shot her a sidelong look. "Nevertheless, the locals

expect it. There would be raised eyebrows, and likely some degree of affront, if I didn't introduce you."

"I see."

Of course, she did. Sawyer was simply performing his duties as earl. And as his countess, she now had her obligations, as well.

"The villagers have all been friendly and welcoming," she added. "And everyone appears to like you."

Sawyer looked amused. "You're surprised?"

She'd heard tales from the locals of his do-good nature, from his initiatives in local eco-friendly improvements to his charitable endeavors.

Aloud, she said, "Perhaps they're seeing only one side of you. The beneficent one."

Sawyer stopped and laughed, swinging her to face him. "And you, I suppose," he said in a low voice, "have seen others?"

She searched his face and remembered last night—seeing him nearly naked and clearly aroused.

"Did you like my other side?" he asked, his voice a caress.

"Why did you leave so abruptly?" she countered.

"Why do you think?" he responded. "If we'd continued, I would have fulfilled your expectation that I wanted to bed you as a novelty."

She was surprised by his forthright answer. "And that isn't what you were looking for when you appeared during my shower?"

His lips quirked. "I'm thinking you're a lot more complex than a novel shag—"

Her eyes widened.

"—and the earl is only one part of who I am."

He held her gaze for a moment longer, and then looked up the street.

She turned, too, and noticed a passerby was approaching. Their private conversation was at an end.

"This is ridiculous."

"Humor me," Sawyer responded, capturing her hand from where he lay on the picnic blanket set near a small duck pond.

It was a glorious summer day, with the occasional puffy cloud drifting overhead, and they had a basket of wine and cheese and French bread with them.

Timing was everything, he thought, and he planned to use this interlude to his advantage.

Tamara looked down at him from her sitting position, her brow puckering. "Everyone thinks this isn't a love match, but a dynastic marriage for mutual advantage—"

"Yes, except they don't know exactly what mutual advantage." He waggled his brows as he rested her hand on his chest. "They think you married me for my money and title—"

"Well, for your money," she conceded.

"—and I've married you to secure Kincaid News."

"Which you all but have."

"True."

Legal due diligence was being performed, and the merger documents were being drawn up. Soon Kincaid News and Melton Media would be one company—if all went according to plan.

"So," Tamara argued, "people are hardly expecting us to act lovey-dovey. Not that Pia and Belinda, or the Marquess of Easterbridge and the Duke of Hawkshire, for that matter, ever had that expectation. And in any case, they've departed."

"Your father and most of the rest of our families remain," he was obliged to point out solemnly. "One can never have too much assurance when you're the father of the bride and are on the verge of parting with your business."

"Then I wonder why my father did it," Tamara countered.

Sawyer shrugged. "He's getting older, and consolidation is the name of the game in the media business these days. In any case, he'll retain a title in the new organization. He'll have power over what remains under the name Kincaid News."

Tamara studied him. "And how do you feel about having my father around?"

Sawyer smiled. "I plan to observe and learn all his tricks."

She shook her head with mock resignation, and Sawyer played with her hand on his chest.

She looked enticing, staring down at him from her position on the blanket. Her dark-red hair caught the summer breeze. An off-the-shoulder crocheted top and short, layered skirt gave her the look of a latter-day peasant girl and accentuated her sensuality.

Sawyer felt his body stir in response.

She didn't look as if she was immune to him, either, dressed as he was in an open-collared white shirt and dark trousers.

But first he knew he had to break down some of her resistance. Due to some perverse streak of nobility, he'd resisted taking her to bed two nights ago. Her hint of vulnerability had done him in. But now he vowed to rectify the matter.

"You're enjoying the English countryside," he remarked.

She nodded. "It's pretty. I've never been to Gloucestershire before. It's inspiring."

He hoped it would inspire her right into his bed, but he settled for arching a brow.

"Not for your jewelry, surely?" he inquired.

She nodded her assent. "The natural beauty is arresting."

"I see." And he did. There was natural beauty right in front of him.

"There's some British in you yet," he joked.

"Scottish," she amended. "Way up north. A different landscape from this."

She slipped her hand from his grasp, and he shifted to his side, propping his head on his bent arm.

"We haven't spoken much about your jewelry business," he said, realizing he was curious. "I know about the hedge-fund wife, but apart from her, who are your clients?"

"You mean, what is my business plan? What are my marketing and promotion efforts?" she joked. "Are you afraid you'll never recover your investment?"

"I already have," he replied glibly, "and in any case, I could afford the loss."

Tamara looked into the distance, at the hills visible beyond where they sat on an expanse of ground within sight of Gantswood Hall.

"I'm an artist, not a businessperson," she said, and shrugged. "I produce what I can by myself, and then exhibit at art shows and specialty boutiques."

She gave a half smile as she gazed back down at him. "You could say my clientele is rich individuals, or at least they're whom I aim for."

"Then you're in luck, since I happen to know a lot of wealthy people."

At her raised eyebrows, he added jokingly, "Of course, if you changed the name of your company to Countess of Melton Designs, you'd add a certain panache."

"I couldn't," she protested. "We'll only be married a short time."

He quirked a brow. "Diane von Furstenberg kept the *von* long after her divorce from the prince."

Tamara laughed. "Okay, yes."

He liked her laugh. She didn't do it very often around him, so it was like catching sight of a shooting star.

"As soon as we return to New York," he said, "we'll hire someone to manage the numbers side of Pink Teddy. And

I'll introduce you to people who'll be curious about your collection."

For a moment, she seemed both surprised and pleased, but then she shrugged. "New York seems a world away right now."

He searched her expression. "Don't we both know it."

A noise came from the direction of the house, and she looked up and shaded her eyes. "My father is heading to the tennis court with your mother, Julia and Jessica."

Sawyer followed her gaze. Everyone, he saw, carried a tennis racket.

"Kincaid is up for a challenge," he remarked. "My mother still plays a superior game of tennis."

"My father's determined to remain in the game, in more ways than one," Tamara countered.

Sawyer looked back at her. "The tennis court was added to the grounds during my father's day, at my mother's insistence."

"Was it part of her plan to deal with her new surroundings?" Tamara asked, dropping the hand that shaded her eyes.

"That and running down to Wimbledon every year," he replied half-jokingly.

"How long did your parents' marriage last?"

"Too long." He trailed a hand along her arm. "But the divorce became final the day before my fifth birthday. I recall the birthday party at Gantswood Hall being a huge affair with ponies, clowns and fireworks. But, of course, no mother. Looking back, I wonder whether the party was as much a celebration of the divorce decree as anything else."

Tamara arched a brow.

"Of course, as the heir," he said, reading her look, "I remained with my father after the separation. My mother was the bolter."

Tamara grimaced. "And your father never remarried."

"There was no need to. He had his heir."

Tamara tilted her head. "You seem to bear no ill will toward your mother."

He gave a brief nod. "I eventually understood my parents' complete incompatibility. My mother was twelve years younger than my father and a rich American debutante impressed by a title. After I was born, she began to long for a jet-set life, while my father was busy with his properties and his newspapers, and remained attached to the traditions set by generations before him."

"But she wed again, obviously," Tamara remarked.

"Once she'd tired of being a divorcée, she married Peter, a widowed Wall Street investment banker." Sawyer's lips twisted ironically. "She then unexpectedly found herself pregnant again at forty-one."

"It's quite a story," Tamara commented.

"There were unexpected benefits from the divorce for me," he said. "If it wasn't for my mother, I would never have received my business degree in the States after finishing up at Cambridge. Her contacts, and those of my stepfather before he died, proved invaluable for expanding my business in New York and beyond."

"You're practically American."

"A dual British and American citizen by birth," he confirmed, though he understood Tamara to be joking about his temperament and disposition rather than his nationality. "You have a lot of curiosity."

Tamara flushed.

"Care to compare notes?" he prompted, smoothing his fingers down her arm in a light caress.

She focused on the movement, and he said innocently, "We're in view of the tennis court."

She hesitated, but then said finally, "My parents divorced when I was seven. I left for New York with my mother. But surely you know that part."

He nodded. He remembered hearing of Viscount Kincaid's divorce when it had occurred.

Tamara's lips lifted with dry humor. "Unlike you, I wasn't the male heir, so I could be spared. My father made two more attempts at marriage and obtaining an heir, but I think he finally gave up."

"I'm surprised he stopped at two more," Sawyer commented with gentle humor.

Tamara lifted her shoulder. "You'd have to ask him why, though I believe three ex-wives and the attendant children began to constitute enough of a burden."

Sawyer chuckled, but then queried softly, "Is that what you were? A burden?"

She looked at him with that amazing crystal-green gaze. "I was never called it, but my father and I don't see eye-to-eye on many issues."

"As the Countess of Melton, you have a title that takes precedence over that of your father's, you know," he pointed out sportingly.

She gave a brief laugh. "I hardly care."

"And yet, here you are enjoying country living, and married to me, fulfilling paternal expectations."

"Only for the short term," she protested.

His eyes crinkled. "Then we should make the most of the time we have."

He tugged her down to him, and caught by surprise, she fell against him.

"What are you doing?" she said breathlessly.

"Tut-tut," he admonished. "We're in full view of the tennis court."

"You do make your antecedents proud," she retorted on a half laugh. "Such capacity for trickery…such an unerring sense of duplicity…"

"Mmm," he agreed. "You forgot 'such a skill for seizing the moment.'"

Then his mouth came down on hers.

Tamara studied the partially finished necklace.

Diamonds and emeralds. She'd pressed her suppliers in the Diamond District until she'd found what she was looking for for Sawyer's commission.

Sawyer was helping her business by giving her a large and lucrative order for jewels...for another woman.

At the thought, Tamara felt a twist in her stomach.

From her seat at her workbench, Tamara looked out the loft window of her former and current place of business and thought about picnicking with Sawyer by the pond.

She and Sawyer had left his Gloucestershire estate for his town house in New York two days ago, the day after their picnic on the grounds of Gantswood Hall.

Remarkably, she'd managed to stay out of his bed. She'd moved into the bedroom adjoining his at the town house, and there she'd stayed.

There hadn't been an attempt at seduction since their idyll by the duck pond.

Of course, the picnic had been all for show—for the benefit of her father and other guests—but the kiss hadn't been.

Tamara touched her fingers to her lips. Sawyer had kissed her thoroughly, as usual making her body hum, and she'd sunk deeper and deeper into their embrace. When she'd finally looked up, it had been to notice they had attracted the attention of their family at the tennis court and of three ducks from the nearby pond.

She'd half expected Sawyer to make an appearance in her bedroom on their last night at Gantswood Hall, but though she'd tossed restlessly until the early hours, he hadn't appeared.

He'd surprised her. Again.

Was he bent on being unpredictable?

Not another novelty shag.

She almost laughed at the thought that Sawyer could have been *her* novelty shag. Certainly, aristocratic media moguls weren't her type. She'd steered clear of Sawyer for years.

But then she'd enjoyed her stay at Gantswood Hall more than she expected. She'd enjoyed Sawyer more than she'd expected, especially now that she'd allowed herself to really talk to him.

They were alike in ways she'd just discovered and previously hadn't permitted herself to admit. They were both the offspring of trans-Atlantic marriages that had ended badly. And they were both connected to two different worlds. She'd been charmed by Gantswood Hall, while Sawyer, she allowed herself to acknowledge, was a New Yorker in his own way. He had a business to run—a very twenty-first century one that wasn't just newspapers and television and radio, but online social networking sites, as well.

And then, on top of it all, she'd been stunned to discover the daredevil that lurked inside the serious and proper aristocratic. His adventures dodging bullets had surprised—no, shocked her. Her own claim to being unconventional—a bit bohemian and with slightly flamboyant fashion sense—just seemed… insignificant in comparison.

And, of course, Sawyer attracted her sexually as no man ever had.

She was afraid she was falling for h—

No, she wouldn't let her mind go there.

L— No, *infatuation* wasn't part of the program.

And yet…

Here they were, *married.* And she had another couple of months at least to try to stay out of Sawyer's bed while the dust settled on the merger of Kincaid News and Melton Media.

Help. She knew all about how oxytocin flooded a woman's

head during sex, bonding her to her sexual partner. Making her think she was in l—

It could only be more so when the sexual partner was already your husband.

Still, she also knew the pitfalls of someone of her background and disposition marrying someone like Sawyer. Didn't she?

Tomorrow, Sawyer would expect her to appear on his arm for a reception and dinner at an Upper East Side consulate to honor visiting European royalty. It was to be their New York debut as a couple.

Did she dare make her first public appearance in a role she'd spent her life avoiding—that of the new Countess of Melton?

Eleven

She came down the town house stairs in a draped strapless emerald dress—folds of fabric crisscrossed her bodice before cascading down in a chiffon skirt. She'd paired the dress with—in a nod to her more unconventional side—peep-toe green satin pumps with feathery bow confections over the vamp. She hadn't had much time to shop for this evening, but fortunately she'd found the perfect dress at the second designer boutique she'd visited.

Sawyer stood at the foot of the stairs, looking every inch the wealthy and powerful aristocrat and media baron.

Frank male appreciation was stamped on his features, and she breathed in deeply to quell the sudden butterflies in her stomach.

Sawyer had knocked on her bedroom door moments before and, when she'd told him she was almost done getting ready, he'd insisted there was something she had to see downstairs.

Stifling a sigh, she'd complied. Her hair had already been

done, thanks to the salon she'd visited earlier in the day, and her makeup had been carefully applied. There really hadn't been much else to do, except dither until the appointed time.

"You look fantastic," Sawyer said now.

"Thank you," she responded.

She wet her lips, and his eyes focused on her mouth.

Sexual tension crackled between them.

She told herself she'd dressed the part of a proper countess in order to convince the world that theirs was a real marriage, and not to please Sawyer. But she knew she was playing a dangerous game.

Sawyer slid a velvet case off a nearby console table. "I wasn't sure how you'd be dressed tonight, but I believe I chose well."

He held the box in front of her, and she swallowed.

He looked amused. "Don't be afraid to open it."

"I thought you'd choose a Pink Teddy creation," she tried gamely.

"And I thought you'd make another exception for the Melton family jewels," he teased, opening the box for her.

She caught sight of the jewelry inside, and her mouth opened in silent surprise.

Nestled on an ivory satin surface was a simple but exquisite tiara made of diamonds and emeralds.

She touched the tip of one tiara point. "It's beautiful."

"Only as beautiful as the intended wearer."

She searched his expression.

The corner of Sawyer's mouth lifted. "After all," he said with a tinge of humor, "if we're going to convince the world we're really married, we might as well play the part to the hilt."

She felt let down at his words, and broke eye contact before he could read her expression.

Of course, this wasn't real. She knew that.

The tiara was real, but the countess wasn't.

She retreated to safe territory. "It reminds me of the Queen Victoria Emerald and Diamond Tiara."

Sawyer smiled. "You're familiar with it? One of my nineteenth-century ancestors liked it so much, she commissioned a tiara in a similar style."

"Well, the Queen Victoria tiara was very famous in its time," she responded, and then touched one of the points on the tiara resting in Sawyer's hands. "It's in what's known as the Gothic Revival style."

"If one tiara gets you this excited," Sawyer teased, "I really should let you play in the family vault."

The sexual suggestion in his comment, accompanied by the look in his eyes, made her heat. And just like that, the air between them became charged again.

"I'm not excited."

"I am," he murmured.

He set the box down and removed the tiara. Carefully, he nestled the jewelry in her hair.

"There," Sawyer murmured.

He admired his handiwork for a moment before his topaz gaze traveled to meet hers.

He bent and brushed a kiss across her lips.

She felt the tingle down to her toes. "I'll be right back," she said, her voice breathless. "I'll have to go anchor it with pins."

Somehow she found her way back upstairs, and with shaky legs, sat down in front of her vanity. How was she going to survive tonight?

Was it gauche to be unable to take your eyes off your wife on your first public appearance as a couple?

If so, Sawyer thought self-deprecatingly, he was as unsophisticated as they came.

But he didn't give a damn. He was impatient to get Tamara home—alone.

Around him, assorted dignitaries and politicians mingled in the reception rooms on the ground floor of the consulate. Later, they'd all ascend to the second floor for a sit-down dinner.

And unfortunately, Tamara seemed to be having a marvelous time and appeared in no hurry to leave. He'd seen her chatting and laughing with two older women whom he knew to be old money pillars of New York society. Then a little while later, he'd seen her fall into conversation with a junior royal as if the two of them had been acquainted for some time.

Already a couple of other guests had stopped to congratulate him on his recent marriage and remark on how charming his wife was and how much they'd enjoyed talking with her and how lucky *he* was.

He'd have dismissed the remarks as idle cocktail party conversation and meaningless flattery, but he'd witnessed Tamara entertaining one conversation partner after another.

It was August in New York, so a sizable portion of the fashionable crowd had decamped to their summer homes in the Hamptons. The crowd tonight was made up mostly of those from the aristocratic and political spheres, with a strong concentration of foreigners. And despite any apprehensions on her part, Tamara was fitting just fine into his social circle.

Sawyer listened with one ear to the two gentlemen with him discussing the economic legislation being debated by the European Union Parliament in Brussels. The rest of his attention was on Tamara across the room, as she chatted amiably with Count de Lyndon, a portly, white-haired gentleman wearing an impressive number of medals and other recognitions on a red sash.

From his vantage point in the consulate's impressive entry, at the foot of the imperial staircase leading to the banquet rooms, Sawyer could easily survey the guests circulating among the various rooms *and* keep an eye on Tamara, her profile to him.

How convenient.

He wondered idly whether Tamara's gown had a zipper at the back or side. He itched to find out.

Damn it.

The bodice of Tamara's gown had fallen a fraction of an inch by the time they'd stepped inside the consulate more than an hour ago, and he'd just been able to make out the top of her rose tattoo.

Now, with laser-sharp vision, he zeroed in on the tattoo again from across the room. The faint outline that he could discern was driving him crazy.

"I say, don't you agree, Melton?"

"Yes, certainly," he responded absently.

"Oh?"

Sawyer's gaze swung back to his companions. The man who'd expressed surprise was the holder of a defunct Eastern European dukedom, as Sawyer recalled.

"You agree that the legislation is a good idea?" the duke asked.

Sawyer glanced at the other man in their circle, a career foreign service officer, who'd posed the original question.

"Any controversy is good for the news business," he hedged.

The duke's face relaxed. "Ah, of course. Rightly said!"

"Will you excuse me, gentlemen?" Sawyer asked. "I've discovered someone I wish to speak with across the room."

His wife.

As he strode toward her, he watched her laugh at something her companion said.

Ever since their wedding day, his desire for Tamara had seemed to grow exponentially. If only there hadn't been that hint of vulnerability that had stopped him on that first night. And then misguided chivalry had taken over. It had somehow seemed *crass* to wed and bed her immediately. He was regretting those scruples now.

Tamara glanced up at him when he joined her and Count de Lyndon. A small smile hovered at her lips.

He longed to kiss her smile, steal it and keep it for his own.

He mentally shrugged at his bit of whimsy.

Lyndon inclined his head, and Sawyer shook the man's hand as they exchanged greetings.

"I wasn't sure you'd be here tonight," Lyndon said heartily. "I half expected you and your lovely bride to be on a honeymoon voyage."

Sawyer threw a quick glance at Tamara. "The honeymoon has been postponed for a more convenient time."

With any luck, he and Tamara would start their honeymoon in earnest in bed later that night.

Sawyer had seen a number of men tonight allow their gazes to linger on her appreciatively. It had made him unaccustomedly possessive, and now he staked his claim.

He rested his hand on the small of Tamara's back as he stepped closer to her. "What have you and Lyndon been discussing, sweetheart?"

From the corner of his eyes, Sawyer noticed Lyndon catch the endearment and smile with knowing amusement.

Good. Let everyone think he was the enamored bridegroom. After all, he had a role to play. That's *all* this was—that and his unfettered lust for his new wife.

"Your wife was enlightening me about the fine art of pottery," Lyndon said.

Sawyer shot Tamara a look of mild surprise.

She lifted a shoulder in a half shrug. "It was a hobby of mine in past years."

"One that I've recently taken up," Lyndon chimed in.

Sawyer looked from Tamara to the older man. "And did she also tell you she is a talented jewelry designer?"

Lyndon chuckled. "Are you, my dear?"

"It's a small business," Tamara allowed.

Sawyer addressed Lyndon. "Your wife may be interested in Tamara's designs. Tamara is making quite a name for herself with her colored gemstone jewelry."

"I shall certainly mention it to Yvonne," the count declared, a twinkle in his eyes. "She does love to be one step ahead of the other ladies."

"As a newsman, I can empathize with the desire to keep ahead of one's competitors," Sawyer said smoothly. "Tamara's studio is located right here in the city—down in SoHo."

"Splendid," the count responded. "Yvonne and I won't be heading to Strasbourg until the end of next week."

From the corner of his eyes, Sawyer noticed Tamara looking at him speculatively, as if she was both astonished and impressed by his seamless plug for her business.

"Your bride is charming, Melton," Lyndon said. "A breath of fresh air in contrast to these women—" he gestured around them dismissively "—who are afraid to get their hands dirty."

The count leaned toward Sawyer as if about to share some confidential information. "She—" he looked at Tamara approvingly "—works with her hands. She even likes gardening!"

"Does she?" Sawyer said, amusement crinkling his eyes. "I'll have to put her to work at Gantswood Hall, then."

Tamara raised her eyebrows. "Really? How much does the gardener earn?"

The count laughed heartily, and clapped Sawyer on the shoulder. "There you go, Melton. Any other woman here would have been decidedly not amused."

"But I am not amused," Tamara protested halfheartedly.

At that moment, another man approached to engage the count, and Sawyer said smoothly, "You don't mind if I steal my wife away, do you, Lyndon?"

"Not at all, not at all," the count responded, waving them away even as Sawyer guided their retreat with his hand at the small of Tamara's back.

When they'd gone a few feet, Tamara asked with slight exasperation, "Do you know everyone? It does seem as if everyone that I've spoken with here knows you."

Sawyer nodded at an acquaintance. "Yes," he acknowledged without vanity, "but the Count de Lyndon is a fifth cousin once removed on my father's side. A female ancestor married into the Belgian aristocracy."

"How charming," Tamara returned, not looking at him either, but smiling as they glided passed a couple of guests and into an adjoining reception room. "You Langsfords have infiltrated bloodlines far and wide."

Sawyer chuckled. "Why not? Queen Victoria and her progeny did it. We had a royal model."

"And you've since been multiplying like bunnies, apparently," Tamara muttered.

Sawyer leaned close and murmured, "Your tattoo is showing above the bodice of your dress."

He caught Tamara's small gasp just before her hand slapped over the spot on her bodice where the tattoo was daring to show itself.

"Are you worried your aristocratic friends will be offended?" she asked tartly, nevertheless matching her low tone to his.

"No," he murmured. "I'm worried they'll want to bed you as much as I do."

Sawyer watched with satisfaction as her skin tinged pink.

Good.

He'd been suffering the temptations of the damned ever since their wedding night, thanks to her. Let her feel some of the heat.

"Are you concerned that I'm being perceived as sexually

available?" Tamara demanded, still refusing to look at him. "Because I can assure you that my behavior tonight has been beyond reproach."

"I see you've misunderstood me," he replied. "You couldn't possibly be more sexually promiscuous than some of the women here."

"Speaking from personal knowledge?"

"I'm in the news business."

"I understand."

"Do you?" he inquired, letting his hand slip to cover her backside and leaning down again so that his mouth was close to her ear. "I wonder."

Her lips parted.

"I'm afraid some here will be consumed by the same inescapable desire I am," he said. "The desire to strip you out of that emerald dress, for example, and make slow and sweet love to you until you cry out my name again and again."

Sawyer watched as Tamara's eyes, focused on the room in front of them, went wide with shock and, yes, a mirroring desire.

She wanted him, too.

She swallowed. "It's hot in here."

"Quite."

She finally looked at him, and her eyes conveyed the same message that was in his. *Let's leave.*

"Tell me you feel faint," he said thickly.

He'd seize *any* excuse she gave him.

"I—"

Unfortunately, they were joined at that moment by the Consulate General.

Sawyer managed to school his expression into a pleasant one as he exchanged greetings and shook hands with the other man.

Damn it. Were he and Tamara destined to be forever interrupted?

* * *

Hours later, Sawyer drove them home in his Mercedes and parked in the private garage next to the town house. Tamara alighted from the car, but before she could take more than a couple of steps, Sawyer came around and took her hand.

Together they walked from the garage directly into the garden and toward the town house itself.

"Did you have a good time?" Sawyer asked, his voice deep.

"Yes," she responded.

She realized with some surprise that she *had* enjoyed herself, despite how unsettled she'd felt thinking about this evening ahead of time.

Tonight, she'd smiled and chatted even as she knew she was comporting herself flawlessly. In fact, she hadn't been sure where Tamara Kincaid had ended and the Countess of Melton had begun. One had blended seamlessly into the other.

On top of it all, a couple of female guests had expressed interest in Pink Teddy creations, and it was only belatedly she'd discovered it had been Sawyer who had extolled her work to them.

His support of her work was oddly touching. Of course, he was probably just looking out for his investment, but still, his encouragement was more than she'd gotten from any man in her life before.

And all along tonight, it was Sawyer's eyes she'd felt. His appreciative gaze had made her acutely aware of her femininity as she'd sipped champagne and tried to concentrate on the conversation around her.

Sawyer stopped in the garden now, and raising their linked hands, placed a kiss on the back of hers. "I'm glad you enjoyed yourself." He bent and brushed a kiss across her lips. "You make a lovely countess."

"Mmm," she responded just before he kissed her again.

When they broke apart, she breathed against his mouth, "What are we doing?"

It had been a magical evening, but she wasn't so far gone on champagne and tiaras not to be lucid enough to ask the question.

Since when, she mused, had *starchy* ceased to be a turnoff for her and started being a powerful aphrodisiac?

Tonight, Sawyer had looked every inch the titled aristocrat born to wealth and privilege—one who, she acknowledged, by dint of his own intelligence and hard work, had expanded the family business to make himself one of the most powerful media tycoons on either side of the Atlantic.

Once upon a time, she would have disdained the aristocrat and not appreciated the executive. But tonight, she'd thrilled to his barest touch and trembled at his heated gaze.

She hadn't been able to help herself.

"I'm giving in to the pull between us," Sawyer said, adding with a note of self-mockery, "We are married, after all."

"An arrangement," she felt compelled to point out.

"One for which we can change the rules at any time."

He kissed the corner of her mouth, and then flattened her hand on his tuxedo shirt, right over his heart.

She felt a flutter, and then another. He was vital and uncompromisingly male.

It was a warm night, the heat of the day fading only a little. Beyond the high wall of the garden, traffic along the nearby avenue stirred the air.

Sawyer eased down the zipper at the back of her dress, and she did nothing to stop him. As her dress sagged against her, and her small satin handbag dropped to the ground, he surveyed her with golden eyes.

She shivered and her nipples hardened further.

"You're irresistible," Sawyer breathed.

She wet her lips. "I didn't think you were paying attention."

"Oh, I was paying attention, all right," he responded, tracing the tattoo that had been exposed near her breast. "This rose has been driving me crazy ever since I first saw it."

At her inquiring look, he added, "While we were dancing at Belinda's wedding reception." He nodded at her now crumpled dress. "Where did this emerald concoction come from?"

"A lucky last-minute find."

"An inspired choice," he modified. "I couldn't keep my eyes off of you all evening."

He bent and covered her nipple with his mouth—a kiss that had her body rising up to meet him as the breath left her lungs.

She held on to his shoulders for support as her head swam. The hard bulge of his arousal pressed against her, exciting her further.

This was *Sawyer. Sawyer.* Her longstanding nemesis. And yet, he made her blood sing, and it was all so delicious. It was a forbidden melding of the proper and the naughty. The oh-so-respectable Earl and Countess of Melton well on their way to coupling outside, unable to keep their hands off each other.

"Sawyer, no. Not here," she said throatily when he finally raised his head to steal a kiss. "Someone at a window might see us."

Her concern was not unfounded. Sawyer's town house sat near several tony white-glove apartment buildings.

"It's dark," he responded gruffly. "And the trees here provide plenty of cover."

"If the media ever get wind of this, you'll never live it down." She added after he stole another kiss, "I can see the headline—'Media Baron Victim of His Own Press.'"

"They wouldn't dare," Sawyer said, but he nevertheless swung her into his arms. "Where to, your ladyship?"

She linked her arms around his neck. "If we're going to be respectable, then I suppose a bed."

Sawyer nodded, and then strode with her toward the house. Minutes later, he kicked open the door to his bedroom.

But instead of laying her on the bed, he set her on her feet and backed her against one of the bedposts. "Let's finish where we were unfortunately interrupted the last time."

Tamara shivered as a vivid image flashed through her mind of their last romantic interlude in his bedroom.

Sawyer undressed her swiftly, following every inch of exposed skin with kisses, and she thrilled with excitement.

Tamara's mind whirled. Familial expectations and everything else receded into the background, and all that mattered was her and Sawyer and what was happening between them in this room.

When he knelt before her and gave her an intimate kiss, the breath left her lungs.

"Oh." She grasped the wood behind her for support, and then as he continued to move his mouth against her, she slid against the cool, notched bedpost pressing against her.

Her climax hit her suddenly and unexpectedly, her back arching, her mouth falling open.

Seconds later, Sawyer straightened, his eyes glittering.

She belatedly realized she was naked while only Sawyer's tie was undone.

He quickly rectified the situation, however, by stripping, and she watched with hooded eyes as he revealed an impressive physique. His erection sprang free of his underwear, and he was finally completely and gloriously naked.

She wet her lips. "I didn't think you buttoned-down types were so…"

He gave her a slow, sexy smile.

Instead of taking her then and there, however, he surprised her by removing the pins from her hair and setting aside the tiara he'd given her earlier in the evening.

She hadn't worn it with any other jewelry, wanting to showcase her one special piece. It had been an unorthodox move, but one that had felt right.

"Hair down this time, Goldilocks," he said.

"I thought you hated the fact that I always let my hair down," she quipped.

He smiled, obviously catching her double meaning. "Maybe I'm loosening up, or maybe I'm a fan of your hair."

Deliberately, he arranged the flowing waves of her hair over her breasts, and then drew the pad of his forefinger over a nipple.

She gasped at the exquisite sensation.

And then he kissed her again. He linked his hands with hers and raised her arms above her head, and guided her instinctively until they both fell on top of the bed.

Sliding his hand down her thigh, he pulled her leg up over his hip, spreading her.

She kissed him hungrily, her fingers flexing on his back.

"I've been told you work well with your hands," Sawyer teased gutturally between kisses. "Show me."

And she did, drawing her palms over him and tangling her fingers in his hair, all the while making love to his mouth until they were both moaning and panting for more.

When Sawyer finally slid inside her, expanding and filling her, she sighed into his mouth with sweet relief.

"Ah, Tamara," he breathed.

She urged him forward, heedless of everything but the primordial urge to copulate.

And he satisfied her, tirelessly, until a sheen of sweat covered his skin, and his unadulterated male scent filled her nostrils.

She gasped, climaxing as he pressed her in just the right spot, and calling his name again and again.

And still he kept going.

She came once more, and then with a shout, Sawyer threw back his head and took his own peak.

Spent, he rolled to the side, taking her with him, and she nestled against him.

Her last thought, before she drifted off to sleep, was that sex with Sawyer had been strangely like finally coming home.

Twelve

He felt great.

He couldn't remember the last time he'd woken so relaxed and...*satisfied*.

Sawyer grinned to himself as he came down the town house steps dressed in black pants and a crisp white shirt left open at the collar. His hair was still damp from his shower.

He would have suggested to Tamara that they shower together, but she'd already been in one of the adjoining bathrooms when he'd woken, and then she'd slipped downstairs while he'd been dressing.

Fortunately, it was Sunday, so he wasn't expected at the office or a meeting. Instead, he knew his chef would have laid out a traditional English breakfast.

He could begin the day in a relatively leisurely manner, though he'd still consulted his BlackBerry upon rising, and his laptop would be waiting for him within easy reach at the dining-room table.

When Sawyer encountered Richard on his way to the dining

room, the butler said with his occasional formality, "Good morning, my lord."

Sawyer smiled easily. "Good morning, Richard. Another hot day, won't you say?"

"Indeed." The butler added, "Her ladyship is already taking brunch in the dining room."

"Excellent. By strange coincidence, it happens to be exactly where I'm headed."

Sawyer was careful to keep his expression bland, but he nevertheless thought he detected a knowing glimmer in the butler's eyes.

When he stepped inside the formal dining room, his eyes immediately connected with Tamara's.

Though the dining room was done in yellow and blue, with brightly striped wallpaper above the wainscoting, Tamara added light to the room.

She was wearing a shimmery sleeveless top, in a coppery color that played off the red of her hair.

"Good morning," he said.

She'd taken a seat near his usual one at the end of the table, and had already helped herself to eggs, toast and coffee.

"Good morning." She seemed to hesitate.

He looked at her thoughtfully. Perhaps she was feeling her way past any uncertainty on the morning after?

Well, he'd have to rectify matters. Before taking his own seat, he bent toward her, and when she looked up automatically, he brushed his lips across hers.

At that moment, André, the chef, brought in a dish of eggs and bacon for him, still warm from the kitchen, saving them from further conversation.

Sawyer helped himself to a scone from a plate already on the table. He was famished, and he smiled to himself when he thought about why.

"Tea?" Tamara inquired.

"Yes, thanks."

Usually, André poured his tea for him. He liked it strong, with a little sugar and no milk.

"Thank you for bringing in breakfast, André," Tamara said as she reached for Sawyer's cup and then a tea bag. "It is delicious. You'll have to share your recipe for these lovely scones."

André smiled. "Thank you, madam."

Sawyer lifted his eyebrows. Of all his household help, his chef was the most reserved and formal. The fact that Tamara had quickly developed a rapport with him spoke volumes.

Sawyer couldn't remember the last time he'd complimented his chef. He paid the man well to prepare his food, and had come to expect as a matter of course that André would perform to his usual high standards.

Seemingly oblivious to his surprise, Tamara poured hot water and added just the right amount of sugar to his tea, and then placed Sawyer's cup and saucer on the table next to his plate.

After Sawyer had taken a bite of his eggs, she nodded at his laptop. "I'm surprised you haven't surfed the news sites already."

"I checked my BlackBerry before coming down," he responded, and then felt his lips twitch. "But thank you for your concern that I not neglect my work."

Normally, he would be engrossed by his laptop, Sawyer admitted to himself, but this morning, he had more enticing distractions. Namely, his wife.

He could think of many pleasurable ways to spend the day with her, but he acknowledged that at least some of those should involve something other than a bed.

Nevertheless, he let his eyes caress her face.

Tamara cleared her throat. "Speaking of your work, I suppose we should talk about where we're heading from here."

There was no need for her to elaborate. His quest to control

Kincaid News had been the motivation behind their marriage of convenience, but they'd arrived at a new status after last night.

"Perhaps we should take things as they come," he hedged with care.

His motivation was becoming tangled, he knew, but he didn't want to examine it. He wasn't clear anymore on how much he was pretending.

He knew the terms of his handshake agreement with Kincaid, but truth be told, last night he hadn't been thinking about the possibility of a pregnancy. Instead, he'd been ruled solely by his desire for Tamara, and the pleasure of making love with her.

Want was merging with need and leaving obligation behind.

Tamara regarded him carefully. "We didn't use any protection."

He raised his eyebrows. "You aren't on the pill or any other contraception?"

She shook her head. "There was no reason to be. Tom and I—"

"—weren't intimate," he finished for her. "Yes, I know."

Sawyer was glad he'd gotten rid of the sad-sack musician. He wasn't Tamara's equal. Sawyer thought that instead she needed someone that was—well, *him*.

More importantly, last night he could have made Tamara pregnant. The thought of a child—his and Tamara's—filled him with profound feeling. He discovered he wasn't averse to the idea at all—far from it—and not only because of his pact with Kincaid.

Still, he knew that for now he had to focus only on overcoming Tamara's trepidations. He'd accomplished the first step of getting Tamara into his bed. He could concern himself later with getting her to agree to dispense with contraception altogether.

"We'll use something from now on," Sawyer said, and then shrugged. "It isn't likely that last night will have...consequences."

"And if there are consequences?" Tamara asked after a pause.

He reached out and ran his hand along Tamara's forearm in a reassuring caress. "We'll work it out." He tried to lighten the mood. "You know, newlyweds have children all the time."

"We aren't like other newlyweds," she disavowed. "We have a business arrangement."

Sawyer felt an unaccustomed prick. "It certainly felt as if we were newlyweds last night."

She looked away, and a pink flush tinged her skin. But when her eyes came back to his, her chin rose. "I spent my life avoiding you—this."

"Likewise," he teased, "but I found that sleeping with the enemy was fantastic."

She arched a brow. "Recharged your batteries, did I?"

Sawyer laughed, glad to see the spirited Tamara back. "Face it, sweetheart. Our charged relationship makes us fantastic in bed."

"Fishing for a compliment?"

He flashed a grin. "For acknowledgment."

He watched her eyes flash, but when she opened her mouth to respond, he laughed and stole a kiss before she could say anything.

Still, when he straightened, she said doubtfully, "This is a bad idea."

He arched a brow.

"Us, as lovers."

Actually, he thought that being Tamara's lover was one of his most outstanding ideas ever.

"Our parents made poor matches."

Too true, he thought with a grimace. Still. "That doesn't have to apply to us."

"How can it not? We've talked about this. Our parents' marriages failed because of incompatibility. The only difference was that my mother wasn't a wealthy American heiress, but a starry-eyed girl from Texas who'd just begun to model."

Sawyer's lips tilted upward. "After last night, I can certainly relate to the urge to give in to desire."

"Exactly, and I'm afraid we'll let—" she waved one hand around "—physical attraction cloud our judgment."

"What a delightful prospect." He looked at her with hooded eyes. "Let's retire upstairs right now and put that proposition to the test."

"Really," she insisted meaningfully.

He sighed and sat back in his chair. "I've met your mother, Tamara, and you two are hardly alike, except—" he paused meaningfully and swept her a look "—you've certainly inherited her model looks and figure."

"Is that my appeal?"

He caught Tamara's guarded expression, which belied her flippant words.

She was afraid of getting hurt.

There it was again—that damned vulnerability that had done him in last time.

Still, he felt strangely tender and protective. "You're beautiful."

And she was. Her green eyes were very expressive of her feelings, and her dark-red hair reflected her firecracker personality.

He'd been around many beautiful women in his life, but there was something special about Tamara.

There'd always been something special about Tamara, he thought, if he'd cared to acknowledge it.

Tamara looked at him, wide-eyed, her eyes like glistening pools. "Oh…"

"Do you want me to show you?" he asked, her emotional

response making him want to push aside his laptop and breakfast, lay her down on the table and demonstrate how beautiful he found her. "You can look as artsy and antiestablishment as you want, but it won't change that you're a beautiful woman."

The air between them became charged with meaning.

"It won't change that you're the daughter of a model from Texas who married a British viscount and media mogul," he went on. "You've also inherited your mother's features and there's nothing you can do about it."

Tamara looked startled at his insight, almost as if she'd never admitted as much to herself.

But she recovered quickly. "Just like your title and hereditary obligations don't change the fact that you're in many ways as American as your name? You're passionate as much as any headstrong American heiress."

He nodded in self-deprecating acknowledgment. "Well said."

She smiled reluctantly, sharing in his humor. "Thank you."

He pushed back his chair and stood. "We're mutts, you and I. Both British and American. In that way, we're more alike than our parents ever were."

"Where are you going?" she asked.

He walked to the door and flipped the lock, and then turned back to survey her.

"Since we're done with breakfast," he said, though neither of them had eaten much, "I thought I'd demonstrate my passionate side again—strictly for the purpose of confirming your assessment, of course."

She looked startled, and then laughed. "Of course."

He moved toward her, undoing the buttons at the top of his shirt.

Tamara pushed back her chair and stood, a small laugh escaping her. "Someone could—"

"—interrupt," he finished for her. "Splendid. Let's start the gossip mill going about what a wonderfully intimate relationship the Earl and Countess of Melton have. After all, that's been the plan all along, hasn't it?"

Frankly, he didn't give a damn about the plan. His only thought right now was what they could do with a dining-room table.

The look he gave her was full of promise before he trapped her against the table, pushed a couple of dishes away with one arm, and bent her backward…

Tamara looked at the stick in her hand, trying to comprehend it.

Two little pink lines should be simple enough to interpret. And yet, her mind refused to grasp what her senses were telling her.

Fortunately, her test kit came with two more sticks. She tried them both, her hand betraying a slight tremor.

Minutes later, there was no mistaking the matter. There were two pink lines of equal intensity.

Emotions chased themselves through her and looped around again. Elation was followed by panic and both were pursued by uncertainty.

She stared at herself in the bathroom mirror.

Five weeks. It had been five weeks since her last period. She had always been regular.

Oh.

She'd only been intimate with Sawyer for three weeks, and this had happened.

Her hand covered her abdomen, over her brown floral print dress cinched by a wide belt.

She'd bought a pregnancy test kit on the way home from work at her SoHo loft. She'd meant to take the test tomorrow morning, after Sawyer departed for work. But once she'd arrived back at the town house, nervous curiosity had overwhelmed her.

She was stunned to realize she was thrilled at the thought of a child…hers and Sawyer's.

These past three weeks had been idyllic. It had been a honeymoon without an official honeymoon. She and Sawyer had laughed, had fun together and grown closer than she'd ever expected. They'd fallen into some of the daily rituals of a married couple, waking together, getting ready for work and attending social functions in the evening.

Unsurprisingly, as the Earl of Melton and a high-profile media mogul, Sawyer received numerous invitations to galas, premieres and parties. And of course, since they were putting themselves forth as the newlywed earl and countess, they accepted many of the invites.

Stepping out as Sawyer's wife had not been a hardship, and, in fact, if she was honest, had served her well. Sawyer's social introductions had already brought more business to Pink Teddy than she would have ever expected.

Sawyer had repeatedly voiced an admiration for her artistic talent in a way that no one—and certainly no man—ever had before. And he'd acted as a sage business advisor—a sounding board who'd offered the services of his own handpicked accountant. For someone who always prided herself on her independence, she was amazed to discover how pleasant it was to face challenges as a team.

And yet…and yet a part of her was terrified.

What would Sawyer's reaction to her pregnancy be? Surprise? Shock? Withdrawal?

Her arrangement with Sawyer was supposed to get her business off the ground. A baby wasn't part of the deal. She knew the reason why Sawyer had married her, and it wasn't so the two of them could have a happily-ever-after.

These past weeks as Sawyer's wife had been pleasurable—she couldn't deny it. But Sawyer had never so much as hinted their sleeping together was anything more than a nice little dividend to their arrangement. He'd never said he loved her.

She felt a pang.

We'll work it out.

Sawyer's words came back to her.

Unexpectedly, he had a chance to make good on his promise. She prayed that his reaction would be all she hoped for and more.

But first, she had to tell him her news.

Tamara checked her watch. It was six in the evening, but she knew Sawyer would still be at his office. He'd told her that he had a late meeting.

Tamara wandered out of the bathroom and into the bedroom that she and Sawyer shared. First, she called her ob-gyn's office to schedule an appointment.

Then she paced. She could wait until Sawyer arrived home, trying to tame her restlessness until then, or she could try to intercept him at work. With any luck, she'd arrive at Melton Media when his meeting was over, or just a little before.

Impulsively, she grabbed her purse from where she'd dropped it on a nearby chair and hurried out of the bedroom. When she reached the town house foyer, she asked Lloyd, who happened to be around to drive her to Melton Media.

Within the hour, she was at Sawyer's offices. Building security recognized her as the new Countess of Melton and waved her by without the need to check in.

She rode the elevator up, and when she reached Sawyer's executive floor, she crossed the reception area, her footsteps muffled by carpeting.

Sawyer's office door was half-open, but just as she was about to peek inside, she froze at the sound of her father's voice coming from within.

"I'm glad to hear most of the due diligence has been completed," her father said.

"My attorneys have said the merger documents will be

ready for our review in the next couple of weeks," Sawyer responded. "Then we can pick a closing date."

Tamara could see neither man from her vantage point, but their words reached her distinctly.

"Splendid," her father replied. "Of course, the deal won't close until I know that you've upheld your part of the bargain and gotten Tamara pregnant."

Tamara sucked in a breath.

"Naturally," Sawyer responded, his tone dry but easy.

She was suspended by shock and disbelief for several moments before realization sunk in, followed by hurt and anger.

She felt as if a boulder had come crashing down on her spirit…and her heart.

The villain.

The double-dealing toad.

She flattened one hand against the office door, pushed and walked inside.

Sawyer's gaze immediately connected with hers from where he sat behind his desk. He rose at the same time that her father swung around in his chair.

Tamara could tell from Sawyer's expression that he'd understood everything about her sudden appearance.

"Tamara—"

"I see I've come at an inconvenient time," she announced, ignoring Sawyer's warning tone.

How dare he warn her. If anything, he was the one who needed to be cautious given how she was feeling at the moment.

Her father belatedly stood, too. "Now, Tamara, I don't know what you heard…"

She held up a silencing hand. "Enough to know that you'll never change. It's Kincaid News you're concerned about first and foremost, isn't it? And it always will be."

Her tone was bitter, but her true rancor was directed at Sawyer, whose face was inscrutable.

"Tell me," she said, willing her voice not to waver as she lowered her hand to clench it at her side, "was any of it real? Or were you faking the emotion even when you slept with me?"

You're beautiful.

He'd seduced her. And she'd fallen for it. *For him.*

Her heart squeezed.

She might not be an ingénue like her mother had been, but she'd nevertheless let herself be swept away by flattery and pretty words.

Her father cleared his throat, his expression grim. "I will leave you and Sawyer to discuss this matter between yourselves."

"Isn't it a little late to decide to stop meddling?" she tossed out as her father made his way to the door.

"Where I come from," her father responded, turning back, "it's called looking out for one's interests, and it's gotten me to where I am, though you and your sisters stubbornly refuse to recognize it."

"I hardly have a choice about recognizing it in this case, do I?" she retorted. "You and your—" she glared at Sawyer "—ilk have seen to it."

Silence reigned then as her father exited the office.

When she heard the office door click, she swung back to face Sawyer.

"All this time I thought you were deceiving my father," she charged, "but I was the one that you were keeping in the dark about the truth, wasn't I?"

Sawyer looked implacable, his eyes flinty. "I was aboveboard with you that day at your loft when I suggested a marriage of convenience. It was only later that Kincaid attached another condition to the merger—"

"And you agreed!"

She took his silence for an admission of the truth.

"I thought you forgot to think about contraception because you were swept up in the moment," she accused. "But you didn't forget, did you? You intentionally didn't ask!"

She'd been swept up in the moment, while *he'd* been planning his next move with the deliberation of a chess master.

The realization stung.

"I was nothing more than a pawn in your game," Tamara said. "All of it was a lie."

Sawyer's jaw set. "Is that what you think?"

"What else can I think? Are you going to deny you deliberately set out to sleep with me?"

"No, I'm not going to deny it."

Tamara lowered her shoulders. *So.*

"I'm not going to deny that I did everything in my power to get you into my bed because I desired you," Sawyer said. "Because whenever I was around you, all I could think about was repeating that first kiss and then some. Because I couldn't get you out of my mind, and I didn't want to."

She shivered, but then steeled herself against his words. Sawyer was an expert at seduction, she reminded herself.

"Why should I believe you?" she demanded. "Why shouldn't I think this is just another ploy to win? You'll do anything to get your hands on Kincaid News, won't you? You'd even seduce your rival's daughter. You're just as ruthless as my father."

"These past few weeks, I'd do anything to get my hands on you," Sawyer shot back, "and as far as I can tell, you felt likewise."

"Yes," she admitted, "and more fool me."

Sawyer stepped toward her, but she raised a hand to ward him off. "Don't, please. There's nothing you can say to make this better for me."

"Tamara—"

"It's over."

Sawyer's tawny eyes kindled, and his stony facade finally cracked. "The devil it is."

"Are you worried about your precious merger falling through?" she demanded accusingly.

"No, damn it," Sawyer said with quiet force.

"I guess this is what they call a Pyrrhic victory," she tossed back, and then spun on her heel and made for the door.

Sawyer didn't attempt to stop her, though some tiny irrational part of her hoped he would.

We'll work it out.

As she hurried to the elevator, she knew there wasn't any way to fix this situation.

Or her heart, either.

Thirteen

Tamara knew that returning to the town house wasn't an option. Instead, telling Lloyd, who was waiting for her outside Sawyer's offices, that she wouldn't need to be chauffeured, she hailed a cab and went straight from Sawyer's building to her SoHo loft.

Once there, she loosened the reins on her hurt and humiliation. Tears pricked her eyes.

What was she going to do?

She stared at the four walls around her. What had she given up to keep this? She'd made a devil's bargain, and now she was alone and pregnant.

She dropped her purse on the glass-topped table and covered her face with her hands.

She took several deep, steadying breaths.

She could handle this. *She could handle Sawyer.* She'd forged her own path in the world.

Dropping her hands, she waited a moment and then picked

up the phone. Pia and Belinda had always been there for her, and she knew they'd lend moral support now.

She tried Pia's number first, and felt some of her tension ebb when her friend picked up.

"Are you in Atlanta?" she asked after an exchange of greetings.

"No, back in New York," Pia responded. "The Atlanta wedding was last weekend."

"Well, I have some news to tell you, but first I'm going to conference in Belinda."

"Okay," Pia said, her tone suddenly curious.

When Tamara reached Belinda, she asked, "Where are you?"

"I'm at the airport. Newark, to be precise. I'm flying out to appraise some artwork."

"I hope you and Pia are sitting down, because I have some news." She paused and took a deep breath. "I'm pregnant."

Pia and Belinda gasped.

"I knew this marriage of convenience with Sawyer was a bad idea!" Belinda said.

Tamara could only silently second that judgment.

"I should have known," Belinda said darkly. "Sawyer is Colin's friend. Those aristocratic types make a woman do what she never dreamed of doing."

Tamara wasn't sure which situation Belinda was talking about—hers or Tamara's own. Maybe both.

"At least I got off with an ill-advised elopement. But pregnancy!" Belinda sighed. "Oh, Tamara."

Tamara imagined her friend chewing her lip, her brow puckered with concern—though Belinda was always warning that frowning caused wrinkles.

"What does Sawyer think?" Pia asked.

"I haven't told him."

"You haven't told him?" Pia repeated.

"It's a good thing I don't often cross paths with Sawyer,"

Belinda said. "I'd hate to be in the position of keeping this from him."

"Are you going to tell Sawyer?" Pia asked, going to the point. "Or should I say, when are you going to tell Sawyer?"

"I'd like to keep this news under wraps until there's no denying the obvious," Tamara announced. "Aren't there celebrities who've hidden their pregnancies until the ninth month?"

She knew that despite everything, she was going to raise this baby. Her hurt and anger right now hadn't altered her feelings about the pregnancy.

"Wow," Pia remarked. "How are you going to keep this, uh, development from Sawyer while you live with him?"

"Simple. I won't have to because I've left him."

"What? *Why?*"

"Apparently, our marriage of convenience wasn't merely convenient," she elaborated. "I was kept in the dark about the fact that Sawyer agreed to my father's condition of a grandchild, or at least a pregnancy, before the merger of Melton Media and Kincaid went through."

For her friends benefit, she quickly outlined what had happened when she'd unexpectedly arrived at Sawyer's offices. Humiliating though it was, she divulged her discovery that Sawyer had agreed to seduce her for his own gain.

"You should have his head on a platter," Belinda declared unequivocally when Tamara was done recounting what had happened.

Tamara couldn't agree more. "If only."

"Maybe you and Sawyer can work it out," Pia surprised her by saying. "You know, for the sake of the baby."

"Stay married, you mean?" Tamara asked incredulously. "Are you joking?"

"I've see you two socialize since you've been married. You glow when you're around him."

Pia's bald statement gave Tamara momentary pause, but everything inside her right now—anger, hurt, pain—made her rebel against it.

"Of course I glow," Tamara responded. "It's what happens when my temper has been lit."

"He can't take his eyes off you," Pia said with quiet certainty. "Trust me. I've observed many couples."

Pia was a romantic, Tamara reminded herself. "Sexual attraction, nothing more," she said succinctly. "Where did I read about how much men think about sex?"

"Probably *Cosmo*."

"Well, on at least one occasion, Sawyer more than thought about it," Belinda quipped.

Tamara felt herself flush. "Yes, well…I'm swearing you both to secrecy."

"Of course," Belinda said. "And if there's anything I can do to help, all you have to do is ask. You know I'd help you and the baby any way I can."

"I second that," Pia said. "But Tamara, what are you going to do?"

It was, Tamara thought, the question of the hour. "Well, for starters, I refuse to be under the same roof as Sawyer," she said. "I'm at the loft, and I'll be staying here for the time being."

"And then?" Pia prompted.

And then…

She hadn't let herself think about it. Though after Sawyer's betrayal, they obviously couldn't continue on together.

Her heart constricted.

"I haven't thought through a plan yet," Tamara admitted, "but Sawyer and I will go our separate ways. It's what we planned all along."

Tamara knew the pain she felt was only a fraction of what she'd feel in the coming days, weeks…years even.

"I don't know," Pia said doubtfully. "What is it you told Belinda recently—I don't see him going away quietly?"

It was closing in on nine in the evening when Sawyer let himself into the town house. Richard, his butler, had the evening off.

It was dark. Quiet. Unaccustomedly so.

He'd grown used to coming home to someone.

Tamara. His wife.

Except now she was gone.

He loosened his tie with one hand.

Tamara hadn't said anything about where she was going when she'd left his office. In New York, she could be any number of places. Hotels, sublets and short-term rentals abounded. She could also be staying with Belinda or Pia.

Damn.

Lloyd had phoned him soon after Tamara had left Sawyer's building, wanting to know if he should wait to drive Sawyer back to the town house.

After some questioning, Sawyer discovered Tamara had waved off the chauffeur as she'd exited his offices, stating that she preferred to take a cab to her next destination.

Sawyer could tell from Lloyd's tone that he was concerned something was amiss between his employers. Nevertheless, not caring that he'd be feeding Lloyd's suspicions, he'd instructed his chauffeur that he'd find his own way home.

Now he faced a house and a future without Tamara.

What a mess.

And most damningly of all, he'd had a hand in creating it.

He wasn't usually one to imbibe, but tonight he felt like drinking himself into a stupor.

His arrangement with Tamara had been for their mutual convenience, but it had become one for their mutual pleasure and enjoyment, as well.

At least, he'd thought so.

In fact, he'd begun to think he and Tamara should stay married. Things were working out well. It had been surprisingly easy to share a bed and a roof with her, which he'd never done with any other woman.

Why rush into a divorce? Instead, he'd begun to think they should take their time and see where things led.

But now, there'd be no wife and no baby.

Paradoxically, he felt the sting of loss for a child that had never come into being. His child and Tamara's.

Quite apart from his deal with Kincaid, Sawyer realized he'd been looking forward to having a child with Tamara—a little girl with her red hair and green eyes, or a child that blended both their features.

An image flashed through his mind of Tamara's face when she'd stepped into his office and interrupted his meeting with Kincaid.

Despite her charged words, she'd looked crushed.

Sawyer cursed under his breath.

He should never have agreed to Kincaid's secret condition. The only reason he had, he admitted to himself now, was because the idea of bedding Tamara had already begun to have irresistible appeal.

When he reached the library, he went straight to the wet bar and mixed himself a Manhattan. Maybe after a couple of drinks, he'd forget Tamara's devastated look in his office.

Sure enough, a couple of hours later, he was slumped in an armchair, sitting in the dark, his tie hanging loose around his neck. He was right where he wanted to be—well on the way to oblivion.

He felt a low, steady throb at his temples, and his gaze came to rest on the blinking light of his phone.

He stared unseeingly at it. He'd noticed the message signal earlier, but had ignored it. He didn't care who it was if it wasn't Tamara—and he knew the message wouldn't be from her.

Now, though, he was far gone enough, and idle enough, he just might believe in a snowball's chance in hell.

So languidly, he picked up the receiver.

After the standard automated voice intoned that the first message had been received at seven o'clock, Sawyer listened to the call.

"Mrs. Langsford, this is Alexis from Dr. Ellis's office," a woman's voice said. "I'm sorry for the confusion, but I inadvertently scheduled you for a day that Dr. Ellis will not be in the office. Please call us to reschedule your obstetrical appointment."

Even through his current haze, Sawyer stiffened, his senses going on alert.

If Tamara had an obstetrical appointment, then that meant...

Pregnant.

The call was either a mistake—had the woman meant to say gynecological appointment?—or Tamara was pregnant.

Sawyer grasped the arm of his leather chair as a mix of emotions roiled him. Shock was followed by exploding joy.

He was going to be a father.

And then his gut tightened and his next thought was, *Hell.* An unholy mess had just deepened into a life-altering event.

Tamara had known she was pregnant, and she hadn't told him. Had she meant to tell him tonight? Instead, she'd left him.

It's over.

His jaw tightened. Like hell.

In the process of fishing her keys out of her purse, Tamara looked up, saw him and froze.

Despite herself, longing and a sweet piercing pain shot through her.

Sawyer looked grim and uncompromising as he dropped

his folded arms and straightened from his position lounging against his car.

Rather than being dressed in a business suit, he was casual in a blue shirt and pants. He was unshaven, and pronounced creases bracketed his mouth.

Why hadn't she noticed him and the car before?

Her only excuse was that the sidewalk had been crowded with lunchtime traffic. People still walked rapidly in both directions, and the curb was congested with street peddlers.

But now, as if the crowd were parting before a mighty personage, he came toward her.

She muttered under her breath, and then fumbled and dropped her keys. She bent to retrieve them, but somehow he was there first.

"Allow me," he said smoothly.

Sawyer picked up the keys from the ground and inserted the correct one in the front door of her building.

"After you," Sawyer said, as he pushed the door open with one hand.

"What are you doing here?" she demanded.

She was the one who'd been wronged, she reminded herself, and yet he was turning the tables on her.

Sawyer quirked a brow and nodded around them. "Do you really want to have this conversation on a busy street?"

"You helm a media company. The last thing you'd want is a public scene."

He smiled mirthlessly. "Try me. There's always a first time. And you'll find different rules apply to the boss."

Her chin jutted out. "Pulling rank?"

"Pulling strings, if I have to," he replied.

"Charming."

"I'm glad you're still impressed by my charm, among my other sterling qualities."

Abruptly, she turned, leaving him to follow her into the vestibule of her building.

"Pressing your case?" she tossed out as they crossed to the elevator and she jabbed a button. "I think we've said all there is to say."

"Hardly," he contradicted, his voice too close for comfort.

Out on the busy street, at least the forcefulness of Sawyer's presence had been muted by the crowd. Here in her building, though, she felt its full, unmitigated effect.

He was big and overpoweringly male, and despite herself, she felt a primitive awareness.

They rode up in the elevator in silence, and then he let them into her loft with her keys.

She should have bristled at his presumption, but the truth was, she admitted to herself with disheartening frankness, if not for Sawyer, Pink Teddy Designs would no longer even exist.

And yet, he didn't own *her*.

She dropped her purse on her desk and turned to face him.

"I have to admit," he said with unreassuring calm, "it didn't occur to me initially to look for you in the most obvious of places. You've surprised me."

She felt her pulse thrum through her veins. "I'm not hiding, Sawyer. I just chose to leave you. Unlike you, I have nothing to hide."

"Don't you?" he said, his facial features tightening, and anger lacing his soft words.

Her chin came up, but she didn't answer him. She wasn't sure she trusted herself to repeat the lie.

Instead, she walked over to her safe and used the combination she'd committed to memory to open it. She kept Pink Teddy's more precious pieces inside.

Since he'd presented her with an opportunity, she thought she'd hand over his purchases to him—perhaps that would convince him that the two of them were really finished.

She retrieved two green felt boxes and walked back toward him. "I've finished the pieces you commissioned."

As she opened the bigger box, her gut twisted. All this time, she'd been working on this project—*his gift to another woman*—and he'd been deceiving her.

She watched now as Sawyer stared at the glittering gems.

She knew what he was seeing. Initially by chance, and then by design, she'd fashioned a necklace with alternating emeralds and diamonds that complemented the Langsford tiara.

She knew she'd outdone herself, though pleasure had mixed with pain as she'd worked, so that the project had become a sweet torment. Presumably, Sawyer's mistress would get the emerald necklace, and in all likelihood, sometime in the future, another woman would wear the Langsford tiara as Sawyer's wife.

The creation of the necklace had been an act of self-flagellation, she admitted to herself. It had perhaps started as a reminder not to fall for Sawyer, but it had evolved from there. Had she been half hoping to foster feelings in him for her? Had she begun to hope she'd be the owner of the jewelry she fashioned?

Except she hadn't counted on becoming pregnant. Except she hadn't known of his ultimate treachery.

His face inscrutable, Sawyer lifted the necklace with one hand, letting the jewels run over his fingers like a waterfall.

Tamara placed the now-empty jewelry box on her work table, and then opened the smaller velvet case.

Emerald earrings immediately caught the light.

In her opinion, the earrings were just as breathtaking as the necklace.

She glanced at Sawyer's face and noticed his eyes had narrowed. Did he see the similarities to the Langsford emerald tiara here, too?

His face unreadable, Sawyer took the case from her. "They're exactly what I was looking for."

A fresh stab of pain shot through her, and she called herself all kinds of fool. "You know what they say. Give the client what they don't know they want."

"Is that what you do?" he asked, setting aside the case with the earrings with what seemed like deceptive calm.

Tamara raised her chin. "Now you can leave."

"I disagree." He quirked a brow. "When were you planning to tell me you're pregnant?"

He said it so quietly she looked at him blankly for a second. He couldn't possibly—

Then she froze. "What makes you ask that?"

"Don't bother to deny it," he said with sudden and quiet force.

She searched his gaze, holding her ground. "And what if I am?"

His eyes locked with hers. "Then a divorce is bloody well off the table. There is no way I'll let anyone call into question the legitimacy of the heir to the earldom."

Of course, Tamara thought with a sinking heart. Even apart from his agreement with her father, Sawyer's concern was with his potential future heir, not with *her.*

"It could be a girl," she pointed out challengingly.

"Regardless." His eyes traveled down her dress, intimate and probing, reminding her all too forcefully of all they'd been to one another.

"How did you find out?" she asked.

His eyes flashed. "A phone message left by the doctor's office. You need to reschedule your appointment."

Tamara closed her eyes briefly. She'd had her home number transferred from the SoHo loft to Sawyer's town house after the wedding. In her turmoil, she couldn't believe she'd forgotten to do something so basic as to call her doctor's office and update her contact information.

So Sawyer knew all, and much earlier than she'd anticipated and hoped. *So much for keeping a secret.* She hadn't even had time to marshal her forces.

She looked at Sawyer challengingly. "This pregnancy doesn't change anything."

"Permit me to disagree. It changes everything."

"All right, it changes everything," she retorted. "I'll never forget that this baby was conceived to fulfill some—" she waved her hand "—deal with my father."

They were too close, furious with each other.

"All those pretty words," she scoffed, "when you were just deceiv—"

He cut her off with a hard kiss, reaching deep into her soul.

She breathed in his musky male scent and sensed the leashed power in him. He caressed her mouth, demanding a response from her that she unwittingly gave.

When he raised his head, he demanded, "Does this feel real to you?"

She stared at him.

He looked uncompromising. "We're not getting a divorce."

She turned away. "I'm not sure the law will let you stop me."

He grasped her arm and swung her back toward him. "I'm not concerned with the letter of the law."

"Oh?" she asked, bracing herself. "Then with what precisely?"

His expression remained implacable. "Try to walk away, and I pull the plug on this—" he glanced around them "—and fight you all the way on custody. Stay married and all this stays yours, along with the title, position and social standing that comes with being my wife."

She gasped at his bluntness.

This wasn't the man who'd made love to her—the man

she'd thought she was coming to know. This was the ruthless media baron who'd grown an empire—a man that her father could admire.

She knew Sawyer could very well follow through on his demands. He paid the rent on her SoHo loft. Moreover, he'd invested in her jewelry business, and had commissioned her most expensive order to date. He'd breathed new life into her company.

While the law might ultimately prove to be on her side, she didn't have many resources to fight him.

"A contested divorce will be long and expensive," he said, as if reading her mind. "And it'll be messy. I can tie you up in court on procedural issues alone. And then you'll still need grounds for a divorce."

"Oh?" she queried, her tone sarcastic. "You don't think your behavior qualifies as unreasonable?"

He smiled without humor. "I see you're familiar with the legal grounds for a divorce."

"Of course," she retorted, her eyes snapping. "My father has been divorced three times!"

"If you insist on going through with a divorce, then the score will be three to one."

She refused to respond to the taunt. She was nothing like her father. True, she'd be a divorcée, but that was a far cry from being a serial groom who let business trump love and family every time.

"The divorce can still happen after the baby is born," she tried. "With this baby, you can lay claim to having fulfilled the terms of your agreement with my father. Kincaid News will be yours. Why contest a divorce?"

"It's simple," he said, his eyes all golden fire. "I want you back in my house. In my bed."

"We don't always get what we want."

Their gazes clashed, the standoff drawing out the tension between them.

Then unexpectedly, he looked down at the necklace he was still holding in his hand.

She'd toiled over it these past weeks, wanting it to be perfect. Thinking about him. What a fool she'd been.

"Here," he said, holding it out to her. "This was always meant for you."

Automatically, she stretched out her hand and took the necklace from him.

"Thank you," she said flippantly, unthinkingly disguising her hurt. "My lawyer will be in touch."

Sawyer's face tightened, and then he turned and strode to the front door. Seconds later, the door slammed shut behind him, the noise reverberating through the loft.

Her confrontation with Sawyer over, energy ebbed out of her like a receding wave.

She sat down heavily on the bar-height chair behind her.

Outside, a car honked. The busy city went on with its life.

She focused unseeingly on the necklace in her grasp, her hand pressing against the cool stones.

This was always meant for you.

She couldn't let herself believe him. She knew better than to trust him.

Fourteen

"Tamara is pregnant."

Sawyer's announcement fell into a lull in his conversation with Hawk and Colin.

It wasn't quite the sudden and unexpected announcement it seemed. They had all been sitting in Colin's majestic penthouse living room for an hour already.

But after a snifter or two of brandy, even the most tightly buttoned of men couldn't be faulted for opening up.

It was a Friday evening, and each of them was still dressed in work attire—though ties had already been loosened or shed.

"Surprising," Hawk finally remarked with a surfeit of understatement.

Colin lifted his tumbler in salute. "Congratulations on your impending fatherhood, Melton."

"Thank you."

There was a pause as all three of them took a swallow from their drinks, toasting the impending arrival.

"You've bested me, Sawyer," Colin remarked. "I eloped. You've made the wife *enceinte*."

Colin's face was inscrutable despite his levity, and Sawyer wondered again at the basis for his friend's incomplete annulment. It was unlike Colin to leave any loose ends.

Sawyer leaned back in his leather chair. "Still, you may discover I'll be following your path to a matrimonial lawyer. If you have a recommendation for a good one, pass it along."

At his position beside the mantel, Hawk raised his eyebrows in surprise.

Colin—seated nearby on a camel-colored leather couch—as usual didn't give anything away with so much as the slightest change of expression.

"Surely you don't mean to divorce Tamara now," Hawk remarked.

"No, but she may intend to divorce me."

"You mean to let this go?"

Sawyer grunted. The hell he did. He'd pushed his way back into Tamara's loft, into her *life,* and demanded she come back to him, backing up his words with the threat of stripping her business from her and an ugly divorce and custody fight.

He pushed aside any misgivings at his heavy-handedness. She'd meant to leave him, and who knew when she would have seen fit to inform him of his impending fatherhood?

Yes, he'd made a mistake by agreeing to Kincaid's secret condition, but two wrongs didn't make a right.

He pushed back the encroaching thought that his actions had smacked of desperation.

"I can suggest an excellent lawyer who will deliver a protracted fight, if necessary," Colin said. "On the other hand, I can't guarantee he'll actually complete the divorce—though, on second thought, isn't that what you want?"

Hawk's eyebrows lifted. "Are you admitting, Colin, that you purposely didn't finalize the annulment of your Vegas wedding?"

"I admit nothing," Colin replied. "Except, of course, for the end result."

Hawk laughed shortly. "You're an enigma, Easterbridge."

Colin merely tipped his head in acknowledgment.

Sawyer's mouth twisted with dry humor, but the smile faded when he thought of his own recent dealings with Tamara.

Were his actions those of a desperate man? After discovering Tamara was pregnant, he'd acted reflexively. He'd tracked her down the next day and given her an ultimatum.

Well done, Melton.

He realized suddenly that Colin and Hawk were looking at him and waiting.

He looked from one to the other of his companions. "Have I missed something?"

"Should we expect to read news of your protracted divorce battle in the *Intelligencer?*" Hawk countered with a question of his own.

"I bloody well hope not," Sawyer responded grimly.

"You're going to persuade Tamara not to divorce you, then?"

Persuade wasn't exactly the right word, Sawyer thought. *Threaten* and *coerce* were more accurate.

"I've talked to her," he responded shortly.

It had been two days since his confrontation with Tamara at the loft, and since then, he'd stubbornly embraced his righteous anger.

"Talked?" Hawk queried now.

"I laid the alternatives out for her." Sawyer's lips thinned. "The ball's in her court."

Hawk said nothing for a moment, and then gave a short bark of laughter. "In other words, you went in all hotheaded." He shook his head slowly, ruefully. "I never thought I'd see the day."

"What?" Sawyer asked irritably.

Hawk traded a glance with Colin. "I never thought I'd see the day you'd lose your head over a woman."

Sawyer gave a grunt.

Was Hawk right? Had he lost his head? Tamara had a way of firing his blood, in more ways than one. He'd never had a woman get under his skin that way.

But he'd lived too long, had borne too much witness to his own parents' divorce, and was too aware of his and Tamara's differences to believe he was in l—

Hell and damn.

The realization hit him like a punch to the stomach.

"I don't see what you know about it, Hawkshire," he nevertheless responded with aristocratic hauteur. "Isn't there a wedding planner somewhere who'd dispute your understanding of women?"

Hawk surprised him by refusing to take the bait, and instead, shrugged. "I've learned a few things since. Or maybe it's just easier to see someone else's situation clearly."

Sawyer remained silent.

Had he lost his grip on reasonable behavior where Tamara was concerned? But then, when had he ever been reasonable about Tamara?

And more importantly, Sawyer thought, what was he going to do about it now that she refused to believe or trust him?

When the loft buzzer sounded, Tamara was expecting a delivery person or perhaps an unexpected client.

It was a Friday evening, but people had been dropping by regularly to visit her studio ever since her engagement and subsequent quick marriage.

She knew she had Sawyer to thank for the buzz.

Sawyer.

No, she wouldn't let her mind go there.

But when she went to the intercom, she discovered it

wasn't a delivery or client. Instead, her father asked to gain entrance.

Without acknowledgment, she hit the button to unlock the building door downstairs, left her front door ajar and then wandered back deeper into the apartment, her arms wrapping around herself.

She turned around only when she heard her father's footsteps and then the loft door closing. She knew she looked peaked from her latest crying jag and lack of sleep, but she didn't care. It was only pregnancy hormones, she told herself.

She eyed her father warily. "What are you doing here?"

As usual, he was dressed in a business suit for the office.

She wasn't sure why she hadn't turned him away. Perhaps because she thought he hadn't truly received his comeuppance. She'd left her ire for Sawyer three days ago, and her father had, advisedly and rather uncharacteristically, beaten a hasty retreat from the field of battle.

Rather than respond directly, her father surveyed her. "You look awful."

"Thank you," she retorted.

"In fact, you remind me of myself during one of my divorces."

"I'm surprised that disposing of a wife affected you that much."

Her father sighed. "I suppose in your eyes I bear a passing resemblance to Henry VIII."

"My only quibble is with the word *passing*."

Her father's lips lifted in barest acknowledgment as he stepped farther into the loft and took a seat in her armchair.

She remained standing.

"I suppose there's much we can quibble about, including the particulars of my divorces, some known, some not."

"I've witnessed enough."

"Perhaps." Her father looked around, his eyes coming to

rest on a nearby display case before looking back at her. "It's quite an inviting space that you have here."

"Thank you. I managed to hold on to it with a devil's bargain."

Her father raised his eyebrows mildly. "Sawyer?"

She nodded. "He covered my rent and then some in return for a short marriage of convenience until the merger went through. Of course, I didn't know you had attached a very significant additional condition." She glared. "How could you?"

Her father sighed. "You never asked me why I wanted this match between you and Sawyer."

"Kincaid News," she responded succinctly.

"True, but the old earl and I also thought you and Sawyer would suit."

She arched a brow. "After the failed marriages that you both experienced?"

Her father shrugged. "Every marriage is different. Your mother's inability to adapt to being a viscountess was just one of the reasons that our marriage didn't work, though it was a major one."

"The other being that your heart belonged to Kincaid News?"

Her father grimaced. "I did do my best to make you appreciate your heritage, both with Kincaid News and the title."

"Yes, you did," she allowed. "But anyone can see that Sawyer and I are—"

"—meant to be together."

She shook her head stubbornly. "Will you do anything to succeed? Sawyer has been *pretending*."

"Then he's a damned fine actor." Her father sighed again. "I've had three wives. Allow me to boast some discernment when it comes to a man being ruled by his passion for a particular woman against all reason."

Tamara almost laughed. True, Sawyer had a surprisingly

passionate side, but he was also a ruthless and calculating operator of the first order.

Much like her father.

"You always accused me of putting Kincaid News first, and that may be so. But Sawyer is a different breed, or at least he's become different." Her father shot her a piercing look. "This isn't about business. Quite clearly he values something else more these days."

"All the evidence is to the contrary," she replied bitterly. "Especially now that victory is in his grasp. In a few short months, he'll be a father."

The minute the words were out of her mouth, Tamara clamped her lips shut.

"Ah, I see," her father said, a twinkle in his eyes. "May I extend my heartiest felicitations?"

"Sawyer didn't tell you?"

Her father shook his head. "No. I imagine he wanted to protect you from further upset."

Her gut twisted. "I suppose making me pregnant is quite enough."

"Sawyer is refusing to go ahead with the merger," her father announced. "Only you can get him to see sense and change his mind."

Tamara's heart clenched. Sawyer was refusing to proceed with the merger? She couldn't fathom it, even as her heart whispered that it was because of her. Because he cared.

Still, she steeled herself—she'd been hurt and betrayed too much already. "Do you really expect me to care?"

Her father scrutinized her face. "I believe you do care, whether you want to or not."

She sniffed. "It'll pass."

Her father grasped the arms of his chair and rose. "If you felt that way about him, you wouldn't be pregnant in the first place."

Tamara opened and closed her mouth.

Her father gave her a little smile. "Perhaps you've met your match." Then he leaned over and peered at the jewelry she had on display inside a glass case. "Your craftsmanship is quite superb. I imagine that with someone at your side handling the business angle, you'll have no problem becoming exactly who you want to be."

"Oh? And who would that be?" she asked challengingly.

Her father surprised her by straightening, and then walking over to her and giving her a quick peck on the cheek. "You'll figure it out. You can keep holding on to bitterness at a perceived wrong, or you can leap with your heart. I may be a serial divorcé, but I also never stopped believing in the leap of faith."

He tapped her nose. "In fact, I made another leap of faith with you and Sawyer. Don't try to prove me wrong for the sake of making a point."

After her father had departed, Tamara was left to ponder his words as she absently moved things about in the loft.

Today had been the closest she and her father had ever come to an honest and forthright conversation. And it was all due to Sawyer, strangely enough.

And Sawyer was calling off the merger.

She supposed she should thank him.

Or stay mad at him.

Or…take a leap of faith.

Tamara stared at the pouring rain beating against her loft windows from her position looking out over the back of her couch. As soon as the thunderstorm let up, she promised herself she'd leave.

She nervously fingered one of the emeralds on the necklace that encircled her neck.

She was going to make the biggest leap of faith of her life today.

She looked down at herself. She'd carefully chosen the

scoop-neck beige knit dress to show off her necklace to its greatest advantage.

A rap sounded at her front door, startling her. She wondered who it might be. Her buzzer hadn't sounded from downstairs.

She crossed the room and checked the peephole. She stilled, but then in the next moment, she opened the door.

Sawyer stood there, wetness clinging to the shoulders of his open trench coat and to his trouser legs.

She hungrily took in the sight of him.

"May I come in?" he asked. "One of your neighbors was kind enough to allow me to follow him into the building."

Silently, she stepped aside, and then shut the door once Sawyer was inside.

Then they stood facing each other. Neither spoke, though the air between them was fraught with tense energy.

She studied his face. It had the same smooth, uncompromising planes as always, but droplets of rain clung to his tawny hair, and his eyes…

The expression in his golden eyes was pure, undisguised longing, and she caught her breath.

He held out some papers in his hand. "These are the documents so far for the proposed merger. Tear them up if you want."

She swallowed hard as she took them from him and placed them aside. "Why?"

He raked his free hand through his damp hair. "Because I can do without Kincaid News, but I can't live without you. Because I've searched for a way to have you trust me, and this is the only way I have left to try to convince you that you matter more."

She sucked in a breath. "Oh, Sawyer."

"I took the wrong tack when I came here the other day," he went on. "But for the record, you still have something that belongs to me."

"What's that?"

He took her hand and guided it until it lay flat against his heart.

Her eyes widened. And then, all of a sudden, her heart began to thud loudly.

Time slowed. From outside, the dim noise of the roaring city could be heard.

Her lips parted, and then closed again.

Emotion clogged her throat. "I—"

"Help me out," Sawyer joked, his voice nevertheless carrying an undercurrent of need.

Instead of replying, she went on tiptoes, pulled his head down to hers and pressed her lips against his mouth.

In response, he banded his arms around her, and opened his mouth over hers.

They kissed in a hot press of need, unable to get enough of each other.

When they came up for air, he looked into her eyes. "I love you."

"Oh, Sawyer." She felt the prick of tears. "I love you, too."

Tenderly, he cupped her face and stroked his thumbs over the dampness near her eyes. "What's this? Tears for me?"

She nodded. "I've been shedding buckets for the past several days." She took a tremulous breath. "In fact, I was coming to see you just as soon as the rain let up."

He looked at her inquiringly.

"My father came here yesterday to tell me you were refusing to go through with the merger, and he had some surprisingly sage advice to deliver with the news."

"Shocking."

She gave a smile at his dry humor. "I thought so, too. Apparently, it was clear to others much sooner than it was to us that we'd suit, quite apart from Kincaid News or Melton Media. He made me begin to think…to hope…"

"Sweetheart." Sawyer lowered his hands as his eyes traveled down to her throat. "Is that why you're wearing the necklace?"

She nodded. "I thought you'd take it as a sign when I showed up on your doorstep. Did you mean it when you said the necklace was always meant for me?"

Her heart squeezed because his answer still mattered.

"Yes," he said, lifting his shoulders with obvious mock regret. "There was no past girlfriend. The jewelry was a ploy to get close to you."

Relief washed over her even as she swatted him. "Oh, you…"

He chuckled as he caught her hand, but then sobered. "I promise, no more deception."

"Yes," she agreed. "I was so hurt and angry when I discovered you had to sleep with me in order to gain control of Kincaid News."

"There was no *had to* about it," he countered. "It was pure want all the way. I may have told myself in the beginning that it was at least partly for the sake of the company, but ever since our first kiss, I'd been fighting my growing desire for you."

"Do you think we'll be able to make it work?"

"What? Our marriage?"

She nodded.

"We have so far."

She gave a small smile. "Do you think the world is ready for a Countess of Melton who sports a tattoo?"

"They already are," he replied, his hand inching up her dress and caressing her thigh. "And they're going to love your jewelry."

She searched his face. "You really want me to continue designing jewelry?"

"Yes, without a doubt. You have a wealth of talent. And on top of it all—" he smiled with secret promise "—I have some jewelry I'd like to commission for a certain woman."

"Oh?" she asked, even as he lowered the zipper on her dress and let it drop to the ground—in the process, doing delicious things to her insides.

"There's a necklace I have in mind for a certain flame-haired, green-eyed entrepreneur."

"Mmm?"

"Yes," he said huskily, trailing a finger down her cleavage. "I have an idea in mind for a large ruby pendant that will come to rest right here."

"Do tell," she said. "I see the beginnings of a wonderful collaboration."

"One of many," he responded.

And then he proceeded to demonstrate exactly how pleasurable their latest collaboration could be.

Epilogue

"This is fast becoming your favorite spot."

Tamara looked up and smiled at Sawyer. She nodded toward the ducks nearby as he sat down next to her on the picnic blanket. "We have to keep up appearances for the ducks. Kiss me."

Sawyer arched a brow, but amusement lurked in his eyes. "I doubt they're expecting us to act all lovey-dovey."

She nodded seriously. "Their sense of well-being depends on it."

"In that case…"

He obliged her with one of his heart-hammering kisses. Afterward, he tucked her into his embrace and nuzzled her temple.

Tamara sighed. She and Sawyer had decided to make as many trips back and forth across the Atlantic as they could until it was no longer possible for her to travel during her pregnancy.

And Gantswood Hall was fast becoming her favorite

retreat. She looked forward to raising children here—and in New York.

She was still finding her way in her role as the Countess of Melton. She trod the line between expectation and her own temperament. But in the way that mattered most, she knew she filled her role exceptionally well—she had Sawyer's love.

"Your father has arrived," Sawyer remarked.

"Oh?"

"Business matters," Sawyer replied shortly.

She nodded. Of course, her father had been thrilled with the news that Tamara and Sawyer had reconciled.

"Not come to gloat again, has he?" she asked, turning her head.

Sawyer laughed. "Maybe that, too."

With a baby on the way, and Sawyer and Tamara so obviously devoted to each other, Viscount Kincaid had declared himself completely satisfied.

Tamara sighed. "Oh, well. Gantswood Hall is a large estate. Let him gloat in the east wing."

Sawyer laughed. "We could have warring factions under the same roof, and it would hardly register in a home the size of Gantswood Hall."

Tamara smiled wistfully. "Speaking of warring factions, I wish Belinda and Pia would resolve their differences with Colin and Hawk. It would be nice to invite our friends here at the same time."

"They'll work out matters," Sawyer said with conviction. "Now kiss me—there's a duck eyeing us."

Tamara laughed and turned for Sawyer's kiss.

Some things were worth more than the most precious gems.

* * * * *

Silhouette Desire

COMING NEXT MONTH

Available October 12, 2010

#2041 ULTIMATUM: MARRIAGE
Ann Major
Man of the Month

#2042 TAMING HER BILLIONAIRE BOSS
Maxine Sullivan
Dynasties: The Jarrods

#2043 CINDERELLA & THE CEO
Maureen Child
Kings of California

#2044 FOR THE SAKE OF THE SECRET CHILD
Yvonne Lindsay
Wed at Any Price

#2045 SAVED BY THE SHEIKH!
Tessa Radley

#2046 FROM BOARDROOM TO WEDDING BED?
Jules Bennett

REQUEST YOUR FREE BOOKS!

2 FREE NOVELS PLUS 2 FREE GIFTS!

Silhouette® Desire®

Passionate, Powerful, Provocative!

YES! Please send me 2 FREE Silhouette Desire® novels and my 2 FREE gifts (gifts are worth about $10). After receiving them, if I don't wish to receive any more books, I can return the shipping statement marked "cancel." If I don't cancel, I will receive 6 brand-new novels every month and be billed just $4.05 per book in the U.S. or $4.74 per book in Canada. That's a saving of at least 15% off the cover price! It's quite a bargain! Shipping and handling is just 50¢ per book.* I understand that accepting the 2 free books and gifts places me under no obligation to buy anything. I can always return a shipment and cancel at any time. Even if I never buy another book, the two free books and gifts are mine to keep forever.

225/326 SDN E5QG

Name	(PLEASE PRINT)	
Address		Apt. #
City	State/Prov.	Zip/Postal Code

Signature (if under 18, a parent or guardian must sign)

Mail to the Silhouette Reader Service:
IN U.S.A.: P.O. Box 1867, Buffalo, NY 14240-1867
IN CANADA: P.O. Box 609, Fort Erie, Ontario L2A 5X3

Not valid for current subscribers to Silhouette Desire books.

Want to try two free books from another line?
Call 1-800-873-8635 or visit www.morefreebooks.com.

* Terms and prices subject to change without notice. Prices do not include applicable taxes. N.Y. residents add applicable sales tax. Canadian residents will be charged applicable provincial taxes and GST. Offer not valid in Quebec. This offer is limited to one order per household. All orders subject to approval. Credit or debit balances in a customer's account(s) may be offset by any other outstanding balance owed by or to the customer. Please allow 4 to 6 weeks for delivery. Offer available while quantities last.

Your Privacy: Silhouette Books is committed to protecting your privacy. Our Privacy Policy is available online at www.eHarlequin.com or upon request from the Reader Service. From time to time we make our lists of customers available to reputable third parties who may have a product or service of interest to you. If you would prefer we not share your name and address, please check here. ☐

Help us get it right—We strive for accurate, respectful and relevant communications. To clarify or modify your communication preferences, visit us at www.ReaderService.com/consumerschoice.

SDES10R

Enjoy a sneak peek at fan favorite Molly O'Keefe's
Harlequin Superromance miniseries,
THE NOTORIOUS O'NEILLS, *with*
TYLER O'NEILL'S REDEMPTION,
available September 2010
only from Harlequin Superromance.

Police chief Juliette Tremblant recognized the shape of the man strolling down the street—in as calm and leisurely fashion as if it were the middle of the day rather than midnight. She slowed her car, convinced her eyes were playing tricks on her. It had been a long time since Tyler O'Neill had been seen in this town.

As she pulled to a stop at the curb, he turned toward her, and her heart about stopped.

"What the hell are you doing here, Tyler?"

"Well, if it isn't Juliette Tremblant." He made his way over to her, then leaned down so he could look her in the eye. He was close enough to touch.

Juliette was not, repeat, *not* going to touch Tyler O'Neill. Not with her fingers. Not with a ten-foot pole. There would be no touching. Which was too bad, since it was the only way she was ever going to convince herself the man standing in front of her—as rumpled and heart-stoppingly handsome now as he'd been at sixteen—was real.

And not a figment of all her furious revenge dreams.

"What are you doing back in Bonne Terre?" she asked.

"The manor is sitting empty," Tyler said and shrugged, as though his arriving out of the blue after ten years was casual. "Seems like someone should be watching over the family home."

"You?" She laughed at the very notion of him being here for any unselfish reason. "Please."

He stared at her for a second, then smiled. Her heart fluttered against her chest—a small mechanical bird powered by that smile.

"You're right." But that cryptic comment was all he offered.

Juliette bit her lip against the other questions.

Why did you go?

Why didn't you write? Call?

What did I do?

But what would be the point? Ten years of silence were all the answer she really needed.

She had sworn off feeling anything for this man long ago. Yet one look at him and all the old hurt and rage resurfaced as though they'd been waiting for the chance. That made her mad.

She put the car in gear, determined not to waste another minute thinking about Tyler O'Neill. "Have a good night, Tyler," she said, liking all the cool "go screw yourself" she managed to fit into those words.

It seems Juliette has an old score to settle with Tyler.
Pick up TYLER O'NEILL'S REDEMPTION
to see how he makes it up to her.
Available September 2010,
only from Harlequin Superromance.